"Who are you?"

Emily asked him, still looking for a ray of hope, for a possible avenue of escape.

A good question, Logan thought wearily. One without a good answer. What could he say? That he was a man who lived in the darkness? A half person who had no family, no past, no name? After all these years, he wasn't entirely sure *who* he was.

"Nobody important," he finally said.

Swiftly reviewing his options, Logan decided it would be best if she thought the worst of him. That way she would obey him—without questions.

"I'm going to let go of you now, Emily. Only don't even try to run. I'm bigger, stronger, faster and meaner than you could ever think of being. Understand?"

Wide, frightened eyes stared back at him as her head dipped in assent. He didn't trust her easy capitulation, but he wasn't prepared for the silk-clad knee that went straight for his groin....

Dear Reader,

There's so much to talk about this month that I hardly know where to begin, so I guess I'll start off with this month's American Hero, Race Latimer, in Kathleen Eagle's *Black Tree Moon*. Race is a smoke jumper, an elite fire fighter who attacks the flames from above. He's also a cocky, hell-raising kind of guy who meets his match in social worker Hannah Quinn. You won't want to miss their story.

We're also highlighting new author Kate Carlton this month, as part of Silhouette's PREMIERE program. In *Kidnapped!*, Kate has created characters you won't soon forget. Talk about on-the-run romance . . . ! Be sure to come along for the ride.

Emilie Richards's *From a Distance* is memorable not just for the way this talented author reunites Stefan and Lindsey Daniels, whose marriage had foundered on the rocky shores of discontent, but for the secondary character she introduces. Alden Fitzpatrick is more than he seems, but in ways most people are not yet ready to deal with. Are you? Read this book—and then look for Alden's story, coming in 1993.

The month continues with Marion Smith Collins's *Baby Magic,* a deeply emotional story of loving, of giving, of the miracles of science and the unpredictability of fate. Two people who'd never expected to share the ups and downs of parenting find themselves in just that position. Join Frances Williams in *Shadows on Satin,* as heroine Lori Castleton returns to the brooding mansion that was once almost her undoing. There she has to confront the specters of her past as well as hero Keith McKinnon, a man who can't bring himself to trust her—even though he loves her. Finally, join Desire author Beverly Barton as she makes her Intimate Moments debut with *This Side of Heaven,* a potent mix of the here and now with the shadowy forces of the past.

In coming months, look for books by such favorite authors as Kathleen Korbel, Dallas Schulze, Rachel Lee and Marilyn Pappano. Here at Silhouette Intimate Moments, we try to make all your reading experiences happy ones.

Yours,

Leslie J. Wainger
Senior Editor and Editorial Coordinator

KIDNAPPED!

Kate
Carlton

Silhouette® INTIMATE MOMENTS®

Published by Silhouette Books New York

America's Publisher of Contemporary Romance

SILHOUETTE BOOKS
300 East 42nd St., New York, N.Y. 10017

KIDNAPPED!

ISBN: 0-373-07454-9

First Silhouette Books printing October 1992

Printed in the U.S.A.

KATE CARLTON

has been making up stories since kindergarten. She got sidetracked for a few years by teaching and raising a family. A hobby junkie, she enjoys dabbling in painting, wood burning and needlework, but reading, and now writing, are her favorite pastimes. A winner of the Southwest Writers Workshop award for best contemporary romance, Kate lives in New Mexico with her husband and two teenagers.

Many thanks—
To my family for believing in my dream.
To Melissa and Leslie for making it possible.

Prologue

"Ghostrider has escaped. Logan has run." Long, meticulously manicured fingers nervously tapped against the black leather case of the scrambler phone as the man waited for the inevitable flood of fury that was sure to follow his stark announcement.

"No kidding." Heavy sarcasm floated through the receiver. "I warned you that this idiotic plan of yours would never work."

The thin man repressed the urge to throw the phone against the wall. Instead, he bunched one hand in the pocket of his suit coat, not caring that he was wrinkling the fine material. He'd been so certain, so positive. It was infuriating to find out he had been wrong. Again. Logan should have had no reason to suspect he was walking into a trap. "It should have worked," the thin man snarled. "It would have worked if only Logan had followed orders."

Harsh, humorless laughter grated in his ear. "Logan only follows orders when it suits him. He probably smelled that setup from a mile away. Why do you think they call him Ghostrider?"

"He's just a man," he snapped back, trying to ignore the rasp of unease inching along his spine. "Not some damn ghost."

"Is he?" the speaker taunted. "Who else but a ghost could vanish into thin air, or be in two places at once?"

The thin man tensed at this reminder that Logan seemed to have about as much substance as a wisp of smoke.

"Your plan never had a chance of working. You never had a chance. And do you know why that is?"

A muscle worked furiously in his pointed jaw as the thin man stared straight ahead, unimpressed by the tastefully decorated book-lined study, uncaring that several people anxiously waited in the other room for his next orders. "No," the thin man finally replied. He listened to the other man's soft chuckle, felt again that tiny slice of fear crawl up his spine.

"Because you constantly underestimate Logan."

The cruel dart struck home as the thin man's fingers tightened around the receiver. "What should we do now?" he asked tightly.

"Find him," came the harsh command. "Chances are he's still in the area."

"Impossible," the thin man retorted. "Odds are, he's long gone by now."

"There you go again—underestimating." The patient, indulgent tone raised the thin man's hackles. "He's around there somewhere. Watching. Because he knows you think he's somewhere else."

Wire-snapping tension and burning anger crackled over the line. And something else, the thin man sensed. Something that he had never associated with the man known by the code name Zeus, the man he had secretly worked for, had hated for the past three years. *Fear.*

"If you know what's good for you, you'll find him. And fast," the speaker warned. "Remember, you're in way too deep to stop now."

Yes, he was deeply into this thing. Way too deep. If he didn't manage to find Logan and . . .

"I'll find Ghostrider."

"You can try. He must be found, along with O'Connel, and the threat to us eliminated. Or heads will roll. *Ours.*"

Smashing the phone back into the case, the thin man flipped the lid and snapped the locks. Oh yes, he would locate both men, he vowed grimly. Pure hate pumped through his veins at the thought of the man known to him only as Logan, the infamous Ghostrider. And he'd make the man sorry he had ever risen from the grave.

Chapter 1

What a disastrous day, Emily Osborn thought as she peered through the bug-spattered windshield of her old, reliable Ford. The quiet residential area just outside of Phoenix seemed overly dark, and the late hour made her feel on edge, made the familiar surroundings seem cloaked in shadows, steeped in danger.

Perhaps she was just tired, Emily reflected as she adjusted the flow of cool air coming from the dashboard of the car. She wasn't often out and about this late—even on a Saturday night.

A fresh wave of fatigue washed over her making her feel limp, drained. The blond hair she had washed this morning felt heavy with dust and was scented with the smell of car exhaust. The light pink blouse and the tan skirt she had donned this morning were now wrinkled, damp and sticky in places.

It was more than being tired, Emily realized. It was disappointment. An early-morning panic call from Brent

Conway, her assistant manager at Emily's Corner, had forced her to delay the start of her vacation. Instead of winging her way across the ocean, she had spent the entire day and most of the evening trying to retrieve the inventory list that had been gobbled up by the newly installed computer in the bookstore.

Perhaps it was fate, she mused. Since the Phoenix area had been suffering through a heat wave for the past several weeks, Luke had thought she was crazy to choose a humid tropical island for the first vacation she had ever taken.

A small smile curled her lips at the thought of her older brother. Tall, blond, wickedly handsome, Luke had been the salvation of what otherwise would have been a dreary, wretched childhood. Rowdy, fiercely independent, with a careless disregard for the things their father had preached, Luke had been a constant disappointment to their strict, religious parents.

Not that she had been much better, Emily thought sadly, pushing back a wisp of hair that had escaped the tight confines of her bun. Turning the corner, she suddenly realized why it was so dark. All the streetlamps were out. Bright light spilled from the Scaffer home, which stood across the street from her bungalow-style house, so at least Emily knew there was electricity to run the air conditioner.

Pulling into the short driveway, she edged the car into the inky blackness of the small garage, thoroughly grateful to be home. A cool shower and a few hours of sleep, and she would finally be able to embark on her vacation. Her bags were already packed and stowed in the trunk of her car. Everything was ready for her to make her great escape.

Odd words to use, she supposed. It sounded as if she were disenchanted with her life.

Emily frowned. For the most part, she was quite satisfied. She owned a business, one that was doing so well she was contemplating opening a second store. She was able to indulge in her passion for books and was financially independent.

A niggling little voice inside reminded her that most people would consider her life dull. Emily dismissed it. So what if she, unlike other women, had reached the age of twenty-eight without the excitement and the thrill of ever having a major romantic entanglement? She was comfortable, content. So what if her life lacked excitement—as her brother constantly reminded her. She had her books to spark her imagination, to put the sizzle into her dreams.

Not bothering to turn on the overhead light, she made her way through the garage. Slipping her key into the lock on the connecting kitchen door, Emily let herself inside. As was her habit, she went to place her briefcase and purse on top of the round table that sat in the alcove with the bay window.

She never made it. Emily gasped in shock when strong arms came from behind. One slid around her chest to pin her arms to her sides as a roughly callused hand was clamped over her mouth. In a heartbeat she was hauled back against a body that was as hard as a block of granite.

Panic raced through her, grabbing her by the throat. Every horror story Emily had ever heard or read about intruders came flooding back to her. Blind panic took over as good sense deserted her. She struggled, even though a small part of her knew that her pitiful attempts to break free were no match for the man's strength. It was a shamefully short bid for escape.

Twisting and turning, her fingers curled into claws as she tried to rake her short nails across the hair-sprinkled arms. Like a band of steel, one of his arms tightened across her chest, forcing the air out of her body. Bright pinpricks of yellow light began to dance before her eyes, and she fought to drag more air into her lungs.

"Stop it. Or I'll hurt you."

Emily went utterly limp. The voice scared her as much as being held so firmly, so tightly against the unmistakably male body. It was deep, cold and commanding and held just a trace of impatience.

"That's much better." Suddenly he moved, dragging her through the kitchen, not hesitating in the short hall as he unerringly made his way to her bedroom. The ugly word *rape* hadn't really crossed her mind. It did so now with a vengeance.

Her legs went wild, and she heard him swear harshly as the heel of her loafer struck his shin. Bending, he used his weight to force her feet flat onto the floor. A dry palm was firmly pressed against her nose and mouth as he subjected her to another of those devastating bear hugs. It was all Emily could manage not to succumb to the blackness that threatened to claim her.

He lifted her easily, keeping the pressure against her breasts as he carried her through the bedroom door. Swiftly covering the short distance over the carpeting, he shoved her against the far wall next to the only window in the room.

As if she were a rag doll, he turned her to face him. That iron bar of an arm was slammed against her throat as he covered her, effectively trapping her between the wall and his rock-hard body.

Heart thudding in her chest, the copper taste of fear in her mouth, Emily concentrated on trying to breathe, on keeping her body upright. Praying she wouldn't pass out, she frantically cast around in her mind trying to recall anything she had learned in her rape prevention class.

The pressure eased against her throat, allowing a trickle of air to flow through. Inhaling deeply, she was disgusted by the flash of gratitude that swept through her.

When nothing else happened, curiosity won over fear, and Emily lifted her eyes. Weak light from the house across the street filtered through the sliver of an opening in the drapes. She clearly saw the dark, full beard that covered the lower half of his angular face and strong neck. Shaggy black hair dipped over the deeply tanned forehead, curled slightly along the collarless shirt that hugged the ropy muscles of the broad shoulders and the sculptured chest.

Emily swallowed, and the pressure immediately returned on her windpipe. Desperately afraid that she would lose consciousness, a small whimper of fear escaped her, which drew the man's attention away from the window. Eyes as cold as hell, as black as sin, bore down into hers.

"If I take my arm away, do you promise not to scream?"

Emily solemnly nodded. She would have promised just about anything to be able to draw a free breath.

He didn't believe her. One corner of his hard mouth lifted in a cynical smile. "I suppose it wouldn't make any difference if you did. No one would hear you. Or do anything about it if they did."

Her heart sank to the pit of her stomach. The Hansons, her neighbors on the left, regularly indulged in screaming matches nearly every Saturday night. Nobody, including herself, had ever done anything about it. Still . . .

"Don't even think about it," came the harshly whispered warning.

Logan didn't need more than the pale light pouring through the partially open curtains to see that the woman was scared. One of the first things he had learned in the game of survival was how to intimidate. Thoroughly. In his line of work, it paid to have people frightened of him.

Distaste soured in his mouth because he had been forced into manhandling this woman. Rather astonishing, he mused with little humor, to find he still had scruples. Maybe it was time to get out of this business—while he still had some left.

Only he couldn't get out now.

What had happened to Jamie? His eyes flickered back to the brightly lit house across the street. Had his old partner fallen into the trap while trying to keep the meeting with him? Had he and Jamie failed to connect because Jamie had recognized the danger? Or had Jamie been behind the setup?

Logan felt instantly torn—between the loyalty he felt toward his old friend and the smart thing to do. He wanted to immediately search for the man, but he knew he had to wait until he got some sort of handle on the situation. It was a tough choice. But he had been making tough choices for years; it was what had kept him alive.

Suddenly, wearily, he realized that he didn't quite care for the man who had been forged by those choices.

"There's money in my purse. Please take it and go."

The half-whispered, thoroughly desperate offer drew his attention back to the woman whose soft, slight body cushioned him. She was more than scared. She was terrified. He didn't want that. People who were terrified were unpredictable—liable to do things they would never think of doing. They were dangerous. To him. To themselves.

"I don't want your money. I just need to use your house."

He could see she didn't believe him. Those round ice-blue eyes that dominated her ashen, oval face couldn't quite meet his. They nervously darted around the room—looking for a ray of hope, for a possible avenue of escape.

"Who are you?"

A good question, Logan thought wearily, one without a good answer. What could he say? That he was a man who lived in the darkness? A half person who had no family, no past, no name? After all these years, he wasn't entirely sure who he was.

"Nobody important."

Swiftly reviewing his options, Logan decided it would be better if she thought the worst of him. That way, she would obey him—without question.

"I'm going to let go of you now. Only don't even try to run. I'm bigger, stronger, faster and meaner than you could ever think of being. Understand?"

Wide, frightened eyes stared back at him as her head dipped in assent. He didn't quite trust her easy capitulation. Moving, Logan braced himself for her inevitable blind rush for the door.

But he wasn't prepared for the silk-clad knee that went straight for his groin. Only carefully honed reflexes saved him as he shifted, taking the blow on the inside of his thigh.

Hooking a leg around the back of her knee, he threw his weight forward. They fell on the bed. Small fists blindly lashed out at him, and Logan grunted as sharp knuckles clipped him soundly on the jaw. Grasping her wrists, he slammed them against the bed.

Harsh, desperate breathing filled the dark room as he gritted his teeth and tried to contain the wriggling woman beneath him. She was as slippery as an eel and as desperate as an animal caught in a trap.

Her back arched as she tried to throw him off, and he felt the softness of her breasts pushing at his chest. Wrapping his legs around her thrashing ones, he used his weight to press her deeper into the bed. Logan felt shocked and disgusted at his body's automatic response to her wild movements; he was actually responding to the feel of that too-thin, yet warm body. The rosy mouth had felt so warm, so vital under his hand. The white-gold hair that had spilled from the prim little bun felt so silky against his arm. He could admire the courage it had taken to fight him, even while he cursed it.

Gazing down at her trembling lips, Logan wondered if they would taste as sweet as they looked. Those innocent ice-blue eyes snapped at him with fury and fear. He felt the frustration, the refusal to admit defeat in every rigid muscle in her body.

An alluring fragrance drifted up, and he inhaled deeply. It wasn't quite enough to overpower the strong smell of fear.

Logan jumped from the bed. Hauling her to her feet, he pulled the woman over to the bathroom that was connected to the bedroom. Grabbing a plush towel from the rack, he shut the door and dropped the towel. Using his foot, he pushed it up against the small space between the door and the tile floor. Only after he was certain that no light could leak out did he reach for the switch.

The painful, sudden intrusion of bright light momentarily blinded Emily. As she blinked furiously, the familiar surroundings of her bathroom finally came into focus. One look at the solid figure dressed in black blocking the door, and she was heartily sorry that clear vision had returned.

He wasn't overly tall. Emily estimated that the top of her head might just reach the mouth nestled in the coarse midnight beard. He wasn't extremely broad, and yet she had felt surprising strength in the lithe body. She would put this man somewhere in his late thirties, despite the absence of gray or silver in the blue-black hair.

His eyes were what grabbed her attention. Ebony eyes, they seemed to absorb every scrap of light. If there was something commanding about his presence, there was something compelling about those eyes. They were the eyes of a Rasputin. Of a Jim Jones. Eyes that could convince a body to do just about anything.

Emily felt a shock of recognition right down to her toes. She had never laid eyes on this man, yet she knew him. He could have been a romantic hero—one who had magically stepped out from the pages of a novel. Impossible, she admonished herself. He was a desperate man, one who had to be enraged by her mindless bid for escape.

But he didn't look particularly angry as he lazily folded his arms over his nicely formed chest and leaned against the door. Emily still jumped when he finally spoke.

"As I see it, I've got two choices. I could tie you up and leave you in the tub for the rest of the night." One hand came up to stroke the heavy beard. "Or you could come to your senses and cooperate, and spend a somewhat more comfortable night on your bed." Dropping his hand, one shoulder lifted in a careless shrug. "It's up to you."

Nervously, she licked her lips. "What do you want?"

His eyes raked over her body, making her extremely sorry for her hastily spoken question. Never had a man been so blatant in his appraisal of her. It made her painfully aware that she did not possess any striking features, that her body was far too thin and unremarkable. That hot, dark survey made her understand just why some women went to such absurd lengths to flaunt their assets. She felt the heat begin to rise in her cheeks.

"I told you. I just want the use of your house. That's all."

"Are you hiding from someone?"

"In a manner of speaking. With any luck at all, I'll be gone in the morning."

"And what about me?"

"I'll leave you in the same condition I found you in. If you do exactly what I tell you."

Emily averted her head, not daring to believe him, wishing with her soul that she could.

He straightened away from the door. "So what's it going to be?"

"I'll...cooperate." She hated herself for her easy capitulation, even though the reasonable part of her said it was the wise, sensible thing to do.

Silently berating herself for her lack of courage, she wasn't prepared for the hand that whipped out and grasped her by the arm. Reaching over, he flipped off the light, plunging them into darkness. Then he opened the door.

A bit roughly, he deposited her on the edge of the bed with a harsh, whispered admonition not to move. Emily was amazed how quickly his eyes must have adjusted to the dark as she watched him rummage around through the things on top of her dresser.

Sharp shards of dread froze her blood when he picked up the set of handcuffs she had bought for Timmy, the son of her part-time clerk at Emily's Corner. They were just a toy, yet she had purchased the set because they were as close as possible to the real thing.

The man looked down at the shiny metal he held in his hand. "Kinky," she heard him murmur. Her eyes widened at the sound of his soft, husky chuckle. "Then I guess I should have expected it, given your choice of reading material." He cast an amused glance at the rack of romance novels lined up on the tall chest of drawers.

The amusement dropped, and he raised his dark, emotionless eyes. "Lay down."

The trembling started in the region of her knees and spread. One hand fluttered up to her throat and uselessly hovered there. "What?"

"I said lay down."

Horrified, she looked at the handcuffs. He was going to chain her to her own bed. There was no way she could allow that to happen.

"No. I won't make it easy for you. I'll fight you every step of the way."

The man uttered a rude, guttural sound and moved. Scrambling to her knees, Emily braced herself for an attack. It never came.

He just stood there, so motionless, he could have been an illusion. Emily held her breath as her heart thundered in her chest.

Fighting the exhaustion that threatened to knock him off his feet, Logan eyed the trembling woman. She believed that he was going to attack her. What else would she think, he reflected, given the way he had pounced on her the moment she had stepped into the door, the way he had dragged her through the house right to her bedroom?

His fingers tightened on the handcuffs. "Look, I haven't slept in over thirty-six hours. I'm bound to doze off before the night is over, and I need to make it as hard as possible for you to escape." One sleek black brow cocked at a cynical angle as his lips twitched. "I'm not really into bondage."

For one brief moment, Emily thought she detected a flash of sympathy, of remorse in the black eyes. It must be a trick of the light. What he was doing was laughing at her.

Anger ate at the edges of her fear. What right did he have to laugh at her?

Some spark of pride made her defiantly tilt her chin. "No."

Chapter 2

Emily expected him to swear, to rage at her. A part of her was braced for him to lunge. Her mouth dropped open when he didn't.

"Why me? Why now?" Under different circumstances, that universal, eternal plea might have made her smile. She flinched when he raised his head; those black eyes held no mercy.

"You've got two choices. You can either lay down on the bed, or you can fight me and risk getting hurt. Either way, the result will still be the same."

Emily chewed on the inside of her cheek in indecision. She had never been a particularly brave soul. Defiance had never come easily. As timid as she was, she knew she would never be able to live with herself if she caved in because of his threat.

Pressing her hands together so that he wouldn't see how badly they were shaking, she shook her head.

He moved so quickly and silently, it took her a moment to realize that he had done so. A second was all he needed.

He sprang, knocking her flat on her back as he used his body to subdue hers. Once again she felt that hard chest come down over hers. Jean-clad legs threaded between hers, rendering her completely immobile. A warm, callused palm and iron fingers encircled her wrist. Giving it a hard jerk, he pulled her arm over her head.

She felt hard metal slide around her wrist, and she flinched as he snapped the cuffs together.

A tiny moan escaped when he slid up and the rigid muscles of his belly brushed against her cheek. The sound of metal clanging against metal as he attached the handcuffs to the rail on her brass bed felt so utterly final.

Emily went limp in defeat. A scream was tearing at her throat, yet she found she was incapable of making a sound when those strong arms lifted her slightly off the bed. Pulling down the blanket, he returned her to the bed.

Eyes tightly closed, she waited for what she was sure would come next. She felt a whisper of a caress against her cheek before his weight was suddenly lifted.

Hearing him move away from the bed did not reassure her. Unable to stand the suspense any longer, Emily opened one eye. The man was back at the window, one shoulder lazily propped up against the wall as he stared out at the night.

Why was he here? Why couldn't he just go now and leave her in peace?

An eternity passed as she warily watched the man. Slowly, Emily discovered a very significant fact. After having sustained a certain level of terror for an extended period of time, it leveled off to an almost acceptable level.

The exhaustion she had experienced earlier gradually stole over her. The clawing terror had drained her of energy. Her eyelids felt heavy and weighted. Every time they drifted closed, she snapped them open again. Only to find that the man at the window hadn't moved. Not a muscle.

He was a complete puzzle to her. What kind of man could go for thirty-six hours without sleep and still be able to stand so quietly, still be so fully, so completely in control?

"Get some sleep," he said suddenly. "I know you don't believe me, but I'm not going to attack you."

There was something soft in the deep voice, something almost sad. Emily felt herself relax. Perhaps she could trust him not to attack her; perhaps he would leave her in the morning. Maybe this was all just a horrible nightmare. One that would be banished with the dawn.

A darkly humorous thought passed through her mind just before sleep finally claimed her. Her brother had always been after her to put some excitement into her life. It seemed fate had taken care of that for her.

Logan knew the instant the woman fell asleep. Not just by the change in her breathing, but by the slow lessening of tension and fear in the room. Only then did he allow himself to relax.

Not entirely. He had learned over the years never to completely relax, and that was what sustained the edge needed to keep himself alive.

Now that the woman was no longer staring at him with those terrified, wounded eyes, Logan studied her. He had been taken off guard by his body's violent reaction to her. Predictable, he supposed, when he'd had her pinned to the bed with that sweet, delectable body pressed to his from chest to thigh.

He had certainly seen more beautiful, more vibrant, more exciting women. With the light hair and the pale, ice-blue eyes, she seemed a rather colorless, mouse of a woman—one who would fade right into the woodwork. Something about her, whether it had been her determination, her unpredictability, or her vulnerability, had reached right down and grabbed him, had struck a chord deep inside.

She looked nothing like the grainy black-and-white photograph that had accompanied the dossier he had gotten from Garibaldi. Her picture had given him the impression of a sour-faced, knees-locked, cold fish of a woman. One who would feel obliged to stock steamy bestsellers on the shelves of her bookstore, yet would only sell them wrapped in brown paper and with a disapproving, disgusted look in her eyes.

Logan had to admit to having experienced a flash of admiration and grudging respect for this woman. Instead of trying to escape, she had gone on the offensive and attacked. That took guts.

Given what he had read about her in the file, he had expected her to whine, to whimper, to beg. That look of determination, of half-fearful defiance when she had informed him that she would fight, was the last thing he had expected.

Wearily, he reached up to scrub furiously at the scratchy, uncomfortable beard. What had been a necessary, but annoying disguise in Panama had become pure torture.

He shifted his attention back to the house across the street. Panama. He almost wished he were back there now. There he had known the dangers. Here, he was flying blind, trying to make sense out of a situation loaded with unknown perils, unseen traps and nameless enemies.

Logan watched as the lights went out at the Scaffers' house—one by one. Not a breath of wind disturbed the lacy fronds of the bush outside of the window. Not a solitary soul could be seen lurking in the shadows. The street was as deserted and quiet as a grave.

That could be an illusion. It was likely that they were out there waiting for him to make a mistake.

Pressing his lips together into a tight line, Logan knew he couldn't screw up. Not this time, not when lives depended upon him, not such innocent lives, but valuable just the same.

A quarter of an hour later Logan felt the exhaustion, his concern over Jamie, catching up with him. If he didn't get a few hours of sleep, he would screw up for sure.

Lying down on the bed, Logan made sure not to brush up against the woman. Staring at the low, sparkled ceiling, he reflected that this seemed like such a cozy, domestic scene—hitting the hay with the little woman.

A cynical, half smile twisted his lips. Right. It was so domestic, what with the little woman handcuffed to her own bed, sleeping like the dead because she had had all her strength sapped by terror. By him.

Through years of practice, Logan was able to push all of those unsettling thoughts aside. Using the tricks he had learned over the years, he emptied his mind and forced himself to relax. In a short while he felt himself drifting into a restless dream-haunted sleep.

It seemed like only a matter of minutes when he opened his eyes—fully awake, fully alert. From the very weak light invading the blue-and-white bedroom, he knew that dawn was just a few minutes away.

He hadn't gotten nearly enough rest, but at least he was fairly certain he wouldn't fall on his face. Stretching, he encountered a soft weight, instantly knowing what had brought him out of his light sleep.

The woman. Fear must have dogged her dreams, making her instinctively seek the warmth of his body. Although hampered by the handcuffs, she had tried to find some security by draping her body over his.

He let his eyes wander over the relaxed, refined features of the woman. No, not the woman, but Emily. He knew her name from the dossier that Control had compiled on her. As a routine precaution, there had been a security check run on the people living in the immediate area of the Scaffer house just to make sure that everyone was exactly who they appeared to be. That way, meetings could be held in private without having to worry about any nasty surprises.

He had gotten one big surprise when Emily had returned to her house last night instead of being far away from here enjoying herself on some sun-drenched beach in Hawaii.

What had happened? Had Garibaldi made a mistake? Or had he?

Reaching up, Logan rubbed his weary eyes. There had been too many of those lately and it was costing him. Dearly.

Easing out of bed, he returned to his silent vigil, wishing that he could slip out of the house before the woman awakened. Unfortunately, the only option he had right now was to stay and wait. Then he would track down Jamie, and find out exactly what in the sweet hell was going on.

* * *

Slowly, Emily drifted out of the hazy fog of sleep. She felt rather disoriented, confused. Perhaps because of the frightening dream she had had last night.

Hard metal dug into her wrist when she tried to move her arm. Her eyes immediately flew to the man still standing by the window.

Dear Lord, she thought, closing her eyes. It hadn't been a dream. He was still in the same position she had seen him in last night. Turning her head slightly, she saw the fresh imprint of his head on the other pillow.

Hot color stole into her cheeks. Emily had never spent the night in the same bed with a man. Not even with Jacob, the staid missionary her parents had picked out as a suitable husband for their embarrassingly thin, painfully shy daughter. The man she had once been engaged to hadn't been interested in staying with her; he had only been angry and ashamed by what they had done.

Emily became aware of a pressing need to use the bathroom. There was a dry, sour taste coating the inside of her mouth, and already it was hot and airless in the room. Her tongue came out to moisten her lips, but before she could speak, the man's head jerked around, pinning her with a impassive stare.

"I need to use the bathroom," she croaked, appalled at the plea in her voice.

He never said a word as he fished the key out of the pocket of his black denim jeans and unlocked the cuffs. Hands splayed on his hips, he looked down at her. "Five minutes. Don't lock the door. It won't do you any good."

Emily scrambled off the bed and flew into the bathroom, her face flaming. So embarrassed by the whole situation, she actually ran the water in the sink, even though the man had to be aware of what she was doing. She was shamed, humiliated by her own bodily functions.

She was, Emily realized, as much a product of her upbringing as her own natural shyness. Her own mother hadn't been able to tell her confused daughter about the normal monthly cycle females experience. Emily had had to learn about it from the outspoken daughter of a neighbor. And sex was a taboo subject in the parsonage. It had been Luke who had clued her in on the birds and the bees.

Highly aware of the time limit, she splashed some cold water on her face and brushed her teeth. She wished she could take a shower. Emily made a face at her reflection. Bathing should be the last thing on her mind. Since she didn't quite believe the man's promise to leave this morning without hurting her, she should be thinking about trying to escape.

Feverishly, she searched the bathroom for a weapon. Ransacking the vanity, she couldn't find a nail file, or a bobby pin, or even a rattail comb. The best she could come up with was an unopened can of mousse.

It was better than nothing. Perhaps, Emily mused, she could get close enough to spray it into his eyes, giving her just enough time to be able to get out of the house. Breaking open the seal, she popped the lid and palmed the can, hiding it alongside her thigh.

Quietly slipping into the bedroom, Emily was relieved when the man never even glanced at her. With his attention focused outside of the window, it would give her an opportunity to change into some fresh clothes— hopefully, before he turned around.

As she reached for the knob on her closet, her eyes flickered over to the closed bedroom door. Something inside of her snapped as all rational thought fled. For once in her life Emily did something impulsive, something foolish and totally unlike herself. She threw open the bedroom door and bolted.

Running down the short hall, Emily made a skidding turn for the living room. She nearly made it. Her hand was on the front door's knob when a fist grabbed the material of her shirt. The shirt ripped as she whirled. A sob escaped as she raised her hand and pointed the nozzle directly at his hooded eyes.

With a blurred motion, an arm flashed out, knocking her hand away. Her entire arm went numb when he brought the blade of his hand down across her wrist. The can of mousse bounced off the carpet, then rolled underneath the couch. Jerking her off her feet, he crushed her against his chest, trapping one arm between them.

"You shouldn't have done that."

Her snarl of frustration swiftly died as she stared into a pair of coldly furious eyes. Fear sliced through her, as a deep dread scrawled into the pit of her stomach. Long, agonizing minutes slipped by until the silence was broken by the shrill ringing of the doorbell.

Immediately, a hand was clamped over her mouth as he carried her back down the hall before the echoes of the chimes had faded. Like lightning, he scooped up the damp towel she had used to wipe her face and stuffed it into the walk-in closet—along with her. He followed, crowding them both behind the hanging clothes, right to the back corner. An iron arm came to band itself under her breasts, pulling her flush against his body.

Why in the world were they hiding? No one was going to come in unless she opened the door, and he wasn't about to let her do that.

Every muscle in her body stiffened in disbelief when she heard the sound of the front door being opened. Her eyes widened when she realized why the man had chosen to hide. He must have thought someone would try to enter the house.

How could he have known? She wouldn't have believed it. The only people who had a key to the house were Luke and Mrs. Billings. This was her brother's week to be at his restaurant up in Flagstaff, and surely her kindly, but nosy next-door neighbor wouldn't think her houseplants needed tending this soon, since Emily was only supposed to have left yesterday for her vacation?

"Not one sound," she heard the whispered warning. Lifting her eyes, she saw the gun he held that had not been in evidence last night. Not for anything would she make a sound.

Sweat beaded up on her forehead, trickled down the back of her neck as she listened to the muted sounds of movement in her living room. Shock widened her eyes as she caught sight of a shadowy form through the louvered closet doors. What on earth was Mrs. Billings up to? There wasn't a single houseplant in her bedroom. Emily was stunned when she heard the sound of drawers being opened, and then the definite snap of the top of the hinged hamper in the bathroom.

Why, that kindly old woman was quietly, systematically searching her house! She had always known the woman next door had more than her share of curiosity, but for Mrs. Billings to actually go through her things when she thought Emily was hundreds of miles away was more than she could have imagined.

The shadowy form moved toward the closet, and Emily felt the hard body behind her grow rigid. Oh no, she thought in horror. Was Mrs. Billings now going to pay for her snooping with her life?

"Dorothea dear. It's Beatrice." Shock upon shock shook Emily at the sound of the spidery voice that came from the living room. It wasn't Beatrice Billings who was searching her house, but Dorothea Scaffer, her neighbor from across the street.

Emily nearly gasped out loud when she clearly heard the very refined, very proper Dorothea Scaffer utter a very unpleasant oath. Mrs. Scaffer's obvious irritation at having her search interrupted should have been amusing. Emily didn't feel like laughing.

"I'm in the bedroom, Bea," Mrs. Scaffer called out as her shadowy form moved away from the closet door. "I thought Emily had left the window open in here."

Even though Dorothea was moving toward the living room, there was no lessening of tension in the man. She could still feel the alertness, the readiness for action.

"You left your scarf over at my house, Dorothea."

"I must be getting senile," Emily heard the woman's muted reply. There was no trace of Mrs. Scaffer's former irritation.

"I do so appreciate your coming over here and checking on dear Emily's plants for me, Dorothea."

"It was no trouble, Bea. No trouble at all."

"I did notice on my way over here that dear Emily left her garage door open. I'm sure no one would try to steal her car, but—"

"Her car?" she heard Dorothea cut in sharply. "I thought you said she was on vacation?"

"Well of course she is. I'm sure that nice Mr. Conway from the store gave Emily a ride to the airport. Frankly, I wondered if he might be going with her."

"Why, Bea! Our Emily would never in a million years travel with a man."

Her cheeks began to burn with humiliation at having to listen to her neighbors gossip about her. Unflatteringly so, too.

"Well I do wish she would find someone. She spends far too much time alone, hardly ever goes out. Though that's not surprising considering her parents and all."

"What in the world do her parents have to do with anything?" Dorothea demanded.

"Two more joyless people you could ever hope to meet. I know he's a man of God and all, but I don't think the Lord ever intended for such a lovely young woman to work all the time and never have any fun. Such a shame. Dear Emily's never had a vacation, you know," Mrs. Billings slyly confided.

If Mrs. Billings said "Dear Emily" one more time in that tone full of pity, she knew she was going to do something drastic. She wanted to sink through the floor. It was bad enough she had to stand and listen to her neighbors openly dissecting her life. To have the man standing behind her hear each and every word was awful. The last thing she wanted or needed was to be the object of pity.

"Well, I'd best be getting back. My arthritis is acting up something fierce today," Mrs. Billings complained.

"Let me walk you home," Emily heard Dorothea offer.

Emily was forced to stand in the closet and listen as the two women walked out the front door. A few minutes later she heard the sound of her garage door being closed.

The man made them stay in the closet for another ten minutes before he pushed Emily out, and dragged her over to roughly deposit her on the bed. She thought she heard him mumble something about "nice neighbors." At the moment she could think of several things she could say about her neighbors, things that would have made her mother wash her mouth out with soap—if Emily had dared to utter them.

Feeling completely degraded by the way her neighbors had openly gossiped about her, Emily dipped her head to stare at the black tennis shoes that were planted in front of her.

"Would you like to tell me what that was all about?"

She didn't jump when he spoke, but much to her horror, Emily felt hot tears pooling in her eyes. She felt helpless when they slid from her cheeks to splash on her trembling hands.

Logan didn't even try to offer her any false comfort. He merely allowed her to wallow in her misery as an awkward silence grew around them. Then, when she seemed to have it under control, he spoke.

"Who else is going to come over to snoop through your house?" he asked with deliberate bluntness. He wanted to call the words back as he watched her cringe, grow visibly smaller.

"No one."

"No husband? No lover? No boyfriend?" he snapped out, knowing full well there wasn't. Even if the nosy women hadn't so cruelly gossiped about her, Logan knew a fair amount about this woman and her neighbors. The information had been given to him when Garibaldi had arranged for the meeting between Jamie and himself to take place at the Scaffers' house.

"No," she answered in a small voice.

"And everyone believes you're on vacation?"

"Yes."

He, too, had thought her house would be empty. It was why he had come here to watch for Jamie when he had sensed that all was not quite what it seemed at the Scaffers' house.

Because he had made a mistake, Logan allowed his anger at himself to get the upper hand. "Then why didn't you go?"

"There was a problem at my store that required my attention."

"What about your parents? Are they liable to drop by to check on things?"

"No. They hardly ever come by. Unless invited." By the terse, clipped tone, Logan concluded that invitations to her parents were few and far between. That touch of bitterness puzzled him, yet he couldn't stop to question her about it.

"And that man, Conway, he believes you're leaving for your vacation today?"

He could see the temptation to lie. Surprisingly enough, she didn't succumb to it. "Yes."

Pushing the button in the doorknob to lock the bedroom door, he returned to the window making sure to keep one eye on the woman hunched miserably on the bed. An unnecessary measure since he was quite certain she wouldn't try to make another run for it. Not when her self-confidence and self-esteem had been shredded by those two old harridans.

As he automatically scanned the street, Logan berated himself for having been taken by surprise when she had bolted through the bedroom door. Shaking his head, Logan raised a hand to rub at the back of his neck. He should have expected that bid for escape. After all, this was the woman who had tried to deliver a very nasty low blow last evening.

Out of the corner of his eyes, he saw her lift a hand to scrub at her cheeks. Logan gritted his teeth against an unexpected feeling of tenderness, of compassion, for this woman. Ruthlessly, he shoved those feelings down and locked them firmly away. This thing wasn't close to being over—not for her, certainly not for him.

Neighborly curiosity hadn't brought the Scaffer woman over here this morning. Plainly, she had been sent to look for any evidence of his presence. Since the Scaffers only did occasional work for Control, they probably weren't solely responsible for setting up the trap to snare him and Jamie. He wasn't even sure if they were aware of the trap; maybe they were innocent pawns being used by someone who was well informed and probably connected to Control.

Whoever was running this show was very shrewd, very clever. And very dangerous. He'd have bet they'd have thought he was as far away from this area as possible by now.

Only they hadn't. They had sent the Scaffer woman over here to cover all the bases. Which meant there was no way he could leave Emily here for them to find.

Swiftly, Logan calculated the risks, realizing that there weren't that many options. Since everyone believed she was gone, Emily was going to have to stay with him a while longer.

"I thought you said you would be gone this morning?" The timid voice broke into his thoughts. Logan turned his head.

A mistake, he realized. He was angry at those two old women, at her, at himself. He wanted to grab her and shake her into showing some of that spunk she had displayed last night.

His breath caught in his throat at the sight of white-gold hair spilling over her slender shoulders as she bent her head. The body under the wrinkled, unflattering clothes looked fragile and entirely feminine.

Logan swallowed. "I said with any luck." He shot her a lopsided, cynical grin. "Something I've been real short on lately."

"So what are you going to do?"

"I'm not going to do anything."

"You're . . . not?"

"Nope. We are. We're leaving."

Despite the man's startling announcement, they did not immediately leave. Emily spent hours sitting on the edge of the bed sweltering as she warily watched him. It was the longest morning she could ever remember spending—more tedious than terrifying.

Around noon, he accompanied her into the kitchen so she could scrounge up something to eat. With a loaf of bread she had unearthed from the freezer, the jar of peanut butter she always had on hand for Luke and the lone jar of jelly from the refrigerator, Emily was able to compile a filling, if mundane meal.

The man didn't seem to mind the plain fare. He ate every bit of the sticky sandwich without a murmur.

Once he had made sure the kitchen was left in the same condition they'd found it, they returned to the bedroom. He had her sit on the commode in the bathroom while he set about shaving off his scraggly beard.

Despite her uncertainty, her fears, it was a thoroughly fascinating process to watch. Not once had she ever watched a man shave. Or had ever been this close to a man who was shirtless—except for the rare times her parents had allowed her to go swimming. Luke had never been allowed to take his shirt off in the parsonage, even on the most blistering of summer days.

It made her feel uncomfortable to sit in the bathroom with this stranger. And strangely excited. Like those times Luke had conned her into doing something a little daring, something that had been against her parents' strict rules. A very unnerving feeling.

Casually he glanced up and caught her gawking at him. A slow smile curved his lips, bringing a wave of hot color to Emily's cheeks.

"What's the matter? Haven't you ever seen a man shave?"

Emily ducked her head. "No."

"Not even your father?"

"He would be horrified if he knew I was in here with you."

That hateful smile widened, and once again she got the impression that he was laughing at her. It was every bit as irritating as the last time.

Emily lifted her head. "Why are you taking me with you?" she demanded as he slapped shaving cream on the coarse beard he had just trimmed.

"I need to buy a few more hours. The minute I let you go, you'll call the police." One corner of his mouth lifted in a half smile. "Don't bother to deny it. That never works."

She shivered. He would, Emily realized with a start, be able to keep her for the next couple of weeks without anyone knowing about it. No one would report her missing, simply because they all thought she was on vacation.

It was a most disturbing thought. Emily twisted her fingers together in her lap. Ordering up a measure of courage, she asked, "What happens to me after you get your time?"

Chapter 3

Logan stared thoughtfully at the woman sitting quietly on the edge of the commode. He'd been wondering when she would get around to asking that.

"I'm going to leave you in an empty apartment. Once I know I'm in the clear, I'll phone a friend to come and release you." He flashed her a tilted smile. "Maybe you can still go on your vacation."

Emily felt her jaw drop. Go on vacation? After this? The man certainly had a warped sense of humor.

"What about your friend? Aren't you afraid he'll get into trouble by helping you?"

"He'll only know about it after the fact. He'll know the best way to handle it."

Emily frowned and shook her head. "That's awfully risky. Why can't you just tie me up and leave me here?"

"I can't. I can't take the chance that your nosy neighbor won't come back to search through your stuff again."

"Are you running from the police?" she asked slowly.

"No, I'm not."

"But why are you hiding? Who are you hiding from?"

Slowly, he swished the disposable razor under the running water. "Believe me, you're far better off not knowing."

"But who are you?" There wasn't a single doubt in Emily's mind that he didn't want to take her with him—anymore than she wanted to go. It was so confusing, the way he seemed to take great pains to frighten her out of her wits, yet at the same time, tried to reassure her.

"You can call me Logan. I'm not a criminal." One corner of his mouth tipped in a wry smile. "Although some people might say different."

Logan grabbed a hand towel, bringing it up to hide a grin. Any fool could see how badly she wanted to believe that; any idiot could see that she needed reassurance.

He had learned a long time ago, had learned the hard way, how easily promises could be broken, how quickly things could go sour. Usually when a person least expected it. The woman was going to have to live with her fear—just a while longer.

Using the can of mousse he had retrieved from underneath the couch, Logan fiddled with his hair, sweeping it back off his forehead until it lay flat on his head. Stepping back, he critically surveyed himself in the mirror.

He looked different. Not completely, but just enough so it would be hard for anyone to recognize him. Looking down at the black denim jeans, Logan frowned. They would have to go.

"You don't by any chance have any men's clothes?"

"I have a few things of my brother's." She ran an assessing look over his partially clad body. Logan felt his reaction immediately with the swift hardening of his body, the quick intake of breath.

"You're a bit shorter than Luke. Leaner." Suddenly, her cheeks flamed as she ducked her head.

Logan's grin softened as he looked down at the white-gold hair hiding her face. So the little mouse had been embarrassed by her scrutiny of his body. Was it possible that she had also been a bit excited by it?

The smile quickly dropped. He hoped not. He was having the devil's own time fighting his own reaction to this woman. He didn't want to fight hers, as well.

Three quarters of an hour later, Emily stood in front of the bathroom mirror. The man had rummaged through her closet, picking out odds and ends—things she would have never dreamed of wearing together. Then he had ordered her to change into them.

She looked different, Emily decided. With the way the man had fixed her hair, she looked ... vital, vibrant.

Emily turned from the mirror. It was just too bad it was an illusion, a lie. She was realistic enough to know that different clothes, a change in hairstyle, wasn't going to change her.

Walking out of the bathroom, she nearly ran into the man. His hands came out to steady her, and Emily felt a sharp sizzle travel through her all the way down to her toes.

Her mouth went dry when she lifted her eyes and caught the hint of fire in the dark eyes, a touch of tenderness. Emily felt her pulse begin to race.

That intense gaze drifted down to her mouth, and she was certain that he was going to kiss her. Emily was horrified that deep down inside, she wanted him to. Desperately. Somehow she had lost some of her fear of this man, had fallen into fascination.

A hot light flared in his eyes, before he quickly banked it. Stepping away, he dropped his hands. Whatever spell she had been under for the last few moments was broken.

"Are you ready to hit the road?"

She was more than ready, Emily thought. She had to get away from him and his compelling eyes. Perhaps once outside there would be an opportunity for her to escape. Although she hadn't been able to outfight him or outrun him, there was a chance that she could outsmart him. A glimmer of a plan formed in her mind as she slowly nodded.

A hot blast of humid air hit them as they stepped out the back door. A quick survey of the surrounding area and Logan was satisfied that he had made the right decision. With the temperature soaring well into the triple-digit range everyone, including the nosy old hag from next door, seemed to be barricaded in their houses in an effort to escape from the blistering heat.

Not that it would make any difference, Logan mused as he wrapped an arm around Emily's shoulders and guided her through the back gate into an alleyway. Surrounded as they were by the high, concrete-block fences, there wasn't much chance that anyone would spot them.

The walk down the alley was taken slowly, cautiously. Pausing at the end, Logan made a swift visual sweep of the area. This was the most critical, most dangerous part of this impromptu operation: they would be most visible, most vulnerable on the walk to where he had left the car.

Not so much as a sleeping dog or a prowling cat could be seen. Scorching rays mercilessly beat down, making the tall palms and the hibiscus bushes look tired and old. Undulating heat waves rose up from the dull gray pavement, washing out the brilliant green of the manicured lawns. It all looked so quiet, so deserted. Logan didn't trust it.

Anyone who'd been sent out to watch for him would be fooled into thinking that he was someone else; he was sure of it.

What he wasn't sure of was Emily. She had been far too docile since that last desperate attempt at escape. Now that she'd had some time to think, time to recoup some of the confidence that had been stripped away by those gossiping old women, he had little doubt that she was planning something.

Keeping a firm grip on her shoulder, he escorted her down the street. He hadn't taken more than a couple of steps before he spotted the innocuous-looking van parked down the way. The vehicle could belong to one of Emily's neighbors, but he doubted it. He would bet that there were several of these strategically parked around the area. Logan's mouth depressed into a thin, grim line.

Turning around would only call attention to them, perhaps even arouse suspicion. There was little left to do but brazen it out. Pressing his fingers into her shoulder, Logan lowered his head and laid his cheek on the crown of her head. A rueful smile curved his lips as he felt Emily stiffen in response to this cozy, too-intimate gesture.

"Relax. And smile," he ordered softly.

Emily complied, stretching her mouth into what she suspected was a pitifully inadequate smile. Any hope that she harbored for escape dimmed as she glanced up and down the quiet street. Even though it was a Sunday, not one child was out and about playing. There weren't any industrious gardeners out tending to their landscapes, either.

How could she attract anyone's attention if everyone was all holed up inside houses?

Her lips tightened in frustration. How exceedingly clever of the man to wait until the overpowering heat had driven everyone indoors. Perhaps, Emily reflected bitterly, she wasn't going to be able to outsmart this man after all.

As he guided her down the sidewalk, she kept alert. Even with the slow pace he had set, they seemed to cover the short distance at an alarmingly fast rate, and Emily felt her spirits plunging.

They were almost to the end of the block passing by a white van when she spotted Mr. Wakely moving out of his garage, a garbage bag clutched in his gnarled hand. The eighty-year-old, slightly stooped gentleman was a special customer at her bookstore, and he was bound to call out a greeting. Hope flared anew as she willed the kindly old man to look their way.

She held her breath as the old man's yellowish-brown eyes flickered over them, only to slide away as he bent to deposit the garbage bag into the underground receptacle. Why, he hadn't recognized her!

Warm, moist breath fastened across the shell of her ear as Logan moved his head to whisper, "I wouldn't do it if I were you."

Emily bit down on the urge to call out a greeting. What had she expected? Even if Mr. Wakely had recognized her, had realized that she needed his help, he wouldn't be a match for a man who was in the prime of his life, who was in superb condition, and who was armed.

His fingers bit into her shoulder. "Good girl. You're doing fine."

She wasn't doing fine, Emily thought in disgust. The only thing she was doing was meekly following this man's orders. She had never felt so frustrated, so utterly powerless.

They eased past her neighbor, and Logan steered them around the corner. They ambled down two more short blocks and another alleyway before he finally brought them to a halt next to a late-model Rabbit that was parked less than a block from her house.

He helped her into the car from the driver's side; Emily flinched when he leaned over her. Once again she felt the bite of metal on her wrist as he placed the handcuff around it. Metal clicked against metal as he secured the other end to the handle of the door.

Emily stared down at her anchored wrist, knowing that she had just lost her last chance for escape.

The thin man nervously paced. He had stayed here far too long—longer than was smart or safe. He hadn't wanted to leave, not if there was a ghost of a chance Logan was still in the area.

He didn't smile at his unintentional pun. To appease Zeus, he had sent the Scaffer woman over to check out the only empty house on the block. He wasn't surprised when she had been unable to find any evidence of Logan's ever having been inside it. Nor had any of his other people scattered about the area found one single indication of the man's presence. Ghostrider had vanished, making the thin man's presence in this house a complete waste of time.

Zeus had been wrong. The logical, sensible thing for Ghostrider to have done was to retreat and regroup, before going on the offensive.

Still, when the thin man glanced at his watch and found it once again time to check in with his people, he scooped up the walkie-talkie lying next to its leather case. One by one, he routinely contacted each and every checkpoint.

"Unit three, come in, over."

"Unit three here, over."

"Anything going on? Over," the thin man asked for yet another time.

"Nah. Dull as dishwater here. Over."

"No one passed by? Over."

"Nobody. Except for a guy and his girl about an hour back. Over."

"And you didn't report it? Over," the thin man asked, his temper barely restrained.

"You're looking for one man, right? Believe me, this guy wasn't him. Over."

"Describe him. Over."

"About six feet. Maybe one-eighty. Tanned. Black hair slicked back. Clean-shaven. Wore a loud flowered shirt and white pants. Sound like your man, Chief? Over."

"No," the thin man replied tersely. "What about the woman with him? Over."

"Blond. About five foot five, but skinny. Real skinny. Had about the best pair of legs I've seen in a long time, though. Over."

The thin man shook his head as he signed off, releasing the side button on the walkie-talkie. It couldn't have been Logan. Ghostrider wouldn't move out in the light of day. He would move in the dead of night. Swiftly. Silently. With deadly purpose.

Nor would he have had the time to recruit anyone's help. Logan was a loner.

A look of hatred passed over his handsome features. He, above all, should know Logan's habits by now. He had heard more about the man's exploits than he cared to—and had learned next to nothing about the man himself.

A ripple of unease skidded down his spine. Logan was no phantom. He was just a man. One that had to be disposed of—as quickly as possible.

They had been aimlessly driving around for two hours, drifting smoothly in and out of the late-afternoon traffic. Emily didn't understand the purpose of such idle wandering. With the windows closed and the air conditioning going full blast, there wasn't a chance she could manage to attract anyone's attention.

Glancing out the window, she realized they were in a residential area near downtown Phoenix, cruising the quiet streets at a slow crawl. Without warning, the man—Logan—guided the compact car over to the curb and killed the engine. Emily stiffened when he casually tossed an arm over the back of the seat.

"Relax. I just need for us to look like a normal couple."

She gave him a vague nod of understanding, totally unable to make herself relax. It was very hard when his fingers were lightly drifting over her bare shoulder. There was an embarrassing tingling feeling in her breasts that tightened her nipples.

One brief glance downward, and Emily groaned. Since he hadn't allowed her to wear a bra, her reaction to this thoughtless, idle caress was clearly visible through the ribbed material of the thin tank top.

A hot wave of color washed into her cheeks. Although she rarely wore a bra, didn't really need one, she wasn't used to displaying herself so blatantly. She felt exposed, vulnerable, even though a quick peek at the man beside her revealed that his eyes were elsewhere.

"Why are we waiting here?"

"I'm checking," he replied, still scanning the area.

Checking for what? "There's nobody around."

"There sure isn't," he calmly agreed. "It sucks."

Emily winced at the crude description. "What's wrong?"

"I was hoping for more people so we'd blend in, be less noticeable." He paused and looked directly at her. "I'm going to need your cooperation."

The request should have amazed her, considering the circumstances. Emily found herself trapped by the intensity of his midnight gaze.

Somewhere in the back of her mind, it registered that this man was handsome. There was a strength in the granite jaw, a determination in the firm mouth that had been hidden by the facial hair. The broad, sharp blade of a nose looked cleaner, more in keeping with the rest of his face.

It was the eyes, though, that lifted the rest of his features out of the ordinary. They were hypnotic, thoroughly devastating when he decided to use them, instead of keeping them cloaked, unreadable. They could lure even a pure woman into following him down the path into temptation.

A shiver raced down her spine that had nothing to do with fear. Desperately, Emily tried to pull herself away from those eyes—before she was lost. "I can't believe you're asking for my help."

"Neither can I." One corner of that beautiful mouth tilted in a rakish grin. "You probably won't believe you're going to help, either."

The tip of her tongue peeked out to moisten lips gone completely dry. "Why should I?"

"Because you want this over and done with just as much as I do."

How was it this man read her so accurately? She did want this whole thing over with—without anyone getting hurt. She had little idea why she didn't want to see the man who called himself Logan hurt—possibly killed. He had scared her, had held her against her will, had kept her helpless. Not once had he really hurt her. There was that one moment last night when he had ordered her to lie down on the bed, when she had heard something different in his voice, seen something soft in his eyes.

Regret.

Emily couldn't seem to shake the feeling that he didn't want to do these things to her. That some sort of dire circumstances were driving him to do them.

She frowned. It all sounded so crazy, yet she still couldn't bring herself to believe that this man was as hard, cold and uncaring as he tried to portray himself.

She was crazy, Emily decided with a small shake of her head. Against all logic, in spite of her fear, she was going to do exactly what he told her to.

"Okay, what do you want me to do?"

After parking the Rabbit in a half-empty lot next to an apartment complex, he leaned over and released her from the handcuffs. Emily had to crawl over the middle console. She barely hesitated slipping her hand into his much larger one as he helped her out of the car.

An iron arm came around her shoulders, gluing her to his side, as one hand idly stroked up and down her arm. As ordered, Emily laid her head on the broad chest, next to his heart. Her own traitorous heart speeded up as she melted against the lean, firm body. They probably looked for all the world like a pair of lovers who could hardly keep their hands off each other—just as Logan had intended them to look.

It was odd, Emily mused as they slowly approached the entrance to the apartment complex, that she almost felt depressed now that the nightmare was nearing an end. It was disheartening to think she might never find the answers, might never know if she had been right about Logan not being a hardened criminal—or totally wrong.

Just as they reached the recessed entrance to the building, Logan—without warning—crowded her up against the inside wall, pressing his body tightly to hers. The nubby stucco poked into her back. It snagged the ribbed material of her tank top as she lifted questioning eyes to him.

"Play along," he commanded in a low, rough whisper. Emily's eyes widened as he lowered his head.

The kiss wasn't anything like she had thought it would be. She had expected it to be a little rough, hard, perhaps even punishing. She had thought the man would take command of her mouth, of her. She wasn't at all prepared for the feather-light touches of his sensuous mouth on her lips, cheek and underneath her ear.

There was softness in this man, she realized with a start. It was in the lips that drifted over her face as they coaxed and teased. It was in the hands that held her so gently, as if she were the most precious thing in the world—someone to be cherished and adored.

"Put your arms around me."

Mindlessly, Emily obeyed. Her hands slid up the front of his shirt to lightly, timidly, settle on the broad shoulders.

"Come on, honey, you can do better than that," she heard him coax as he nuzzled her ear.

A shiver of pleasure slipped down her spine. It was pure insanity to wish for one moment that it was true, that she actually meant something special to this man.

"Just close your eyes and hold on to me. Like you couldn't bear to let me go."

Automatically, her lashes fluttered down. Her arms twined around his whipcord-lean body. And when his mouth found hers, Emily felt the world falling away.

He teased and taunted, until she felt her lips relax as they softened and parted. That rough, moist tongue didn't invade her mouth. He used it to explore, flicking it lightly over the edges of her teeth, the roof of her mouth, the inside of her cheeks.

He was tasting her, Emily suddenly realized. One hand came up to encircle her neck, one callused thumb brushed lightly at the soft flesh under her chin. He changed the position of his head, angling it to deepen the kiss, turning it from playfully seductive to deadly serious.

A sound that was suspiciously like a whimper escaped her. The whole world instantly narrowed down to encapsulate just the two of them. She could no longer hear the traffic coming off the busy side street, nor the amused comments of some passersby. Emily felt lost, swamped by feelings, caught up in this man, and the foreign sensations he so effortlessly aroused in her.

Never in her whole life had a man kissed her this way. Singlemindedly. So determinedly. As though he couldn't get enough of the taste of her; as though he would never be able to let her go.

And never had a man made her feel this way, shivery, yet hot as flames, dizzy, and floating inches above the ground. Emily was totally immersed in the startlingly new sensations of touch and taste. She could easily lose herself in the strong, hard body, the soft, warm lips, the heady, sweet taste of Logan.

He suddenly tore his mouth away. Confused, Emily opened her eyes only to be caught in the intense, glittering fire that burned in his eyes. He swore softly, hoarsely.

"Well, I never!"

The words jerked Emily's eyes over Logan's shoulder. They collided with the disapproving look of an elderly couple who were coming out of the apartment complex.

Emily's faced flamed as she buried it against Logan's shoulder. Good Lord! She could hardly believe what she had just done. She had responded to that kiss as if she had been a desperate, love-starved woman. She had allowed this man to kiss the socks off her—without one word of protest. A man who had terrified her, humiliated her and held her against her will. And she had enjoyed it. Thoroughly.

"For a prim little thing, you sure know how to melt a man's shorts." His thumb drifted over her lips, urging her to look at him. "Let's go." The cold, harsh tone was in direct contrast to the hot passionate look he gave her.

Emily didn't understand that Logan was berating himself. Harshly.

* * *

He was furious with himself. It was supposed to have been a simple kiss, one to lend credence to the parts they were playing, for the men he had spotted who were watching them. It was to have been a diversion, a sleight-of-hand trick, so that anyone watching would remember the clothes, the action, yet would be totally unable to identify the players. He had done it before, coldly, deliberately and with a clear head.

Logan certainly never expected to lose it like that. To get so hot, so hard, so quickly, that all he could think of was stripping her out of those clothes to get down to the sweet promise of the feminine flesh.

As he steered them toward the staircase, Logan felt like something that would be distastefully scraped off the bottom of a shoe. The cold professional detachment that always gave him the edge, that was so vital to his work and his survival, had taken a hike. He had immediately spotted the two men in the car across the street, assumed they had been sent to watch for Jamie in case his friend returned to his apartment.

Once he'd had Emily in his arms, once his mouth had found hers, he had forgotten the men who hunted him—a mistake that might cost him far more than he was willing to pay.

Pausing by a door on the second floor, Logan set Emily against the wall, and reached into the back pocket of his pants to fish out his bag of tricks. Opening the walletlike folder, he extracted a metal pick. Just one of many that could get him through all but the most complicated of locks.

Inserting the thin rod, he turned it round, felt a click. He was amazed how easily it opened. It astounded him how a man in Jamie O'Connel's business could rely on such a flimsy, inadequate lock to protect his home, his possessions, his person.

Guiding Emily through the open door, Logan sensed something was wrong the minute he stepped inside. The place had a hollow ring indicating they were alone. Or were they?

The minute he released her, Emily stepped away from Logan and rubbed the spot on her wrist where he had held her. Her eyes nervously flickered over a room that looked more like a motel room than someone's home.

The drab, serviceable furniture had been unimaginatively arranged. No plants or personal touches had been added to give any indication of what kind of person lived here. No picture were hung to soften the stark beige walls.

Her gaze warily drifted back to Logan and stopped. With his head held high, his nose pointed in the air, he looked like an animal scenting danger. Or a predator sniffing out his prey. Emily shuddered at the look of pure ruthlessness she saw in his black eyes.

"Is something wrong?" she forced herself to ask.

Once again he grasped her by the wrist and pulled her toward a door off the shallow hall. Poking his head inside the doorway, he took a quick look around before thrusting her into the room.

"Stay here," he ordered. Emily gazed into a room that was as uninteresting as the one they had just left. The drapes had been drawn, perhaps to keep out the late-afternoon heat. Even in the dim light, she could see that the decor matched that of the front room.

Not a thing was out of place. No carelessly left shoe marred the mud-brown carpet, no personal articles cluttered the top of the dresser. Even though a fine film of dust lay over the furniture, the rest of the room was as neat as a pin.

Her gaze fell on the brown spread covering the sagging bed before drifting back over to the closed drapes. For one brief moment, Emily toyed with the idea of going over and trying to capture someone's attention.

It probably wouldn't do any good, she decided in defeat. With her luck, the window would overlook the alleyway she had spotted beside the building. Or the deserted parking lot.

Hovering in the middle of the room, she caught sight of something out of the corner of her eye. Something that looked pale against the dark carpet. The only thing in the room that looked out of place.

Peering closer, Emily's breath caught in her throat. That something turned out to be a hand. A man's hand, presumably attached to a man's body.

She shook her head in bafflement, wondering why Logan's friend would choose to take a nap on the uncomfortable carpet when there was a bed right beside him.

Cautiously, Emily inched closer, wondering if she should take a peek at the man or go get Logan. Curiosity won out as she craned her neck over the edge of the bed for a better look.

Her heart thundered in her chest as the nasty taste of fear filled her mouth. This man was not taking a nap on the floor. He was stone-cold dead.

Chapter 4

Just as Logan spied the metal disk nestled in the mouthpiece of the phone, he heard a quiet sound of distress. He raced into the bedroom. Spotting a white-faced Emily, his eyes raked over the room searching for any signs of danger. It took him only a second to spot the hand.

It was like taking a two by four to the gut. *Dear God no,* a small voice inside him cried out. *Not Jamie. Please don't let this be the reason his old friend hadn't made it to the meeting last night.*

He let none of his fear or inner turmoil show on his face. Relief hit him hot and hard when he looked over the edge of the bed at the body below.

Not Jamie, he realized, carefully looking over the body. Something wasn't right, and Logan frowned. There should have been more blood. There should have been more of everything when the face had been so messily rearranged by a very large caliber bullet discharged at close range.

Which meant this man had been killed elsewhere, and then dumped in Jamie's apartment.

A barely audible sound drew his attention back to Emily. He felt a painful twist inside when he noted the ashen hue of her face. Her eyes looked dull, lifeless and glazed over in shock.

Instinctively, he reached out to pull her into his arms. He pressed her head against his shoulder, covering her eyes. This was probably the first dead body she had ever seen—up close and personal.

"Don't look," he commanded when she tried to shift her head. "Don't even think about it."

At that moment, he hated himself for so rudely introducing this innocent woman to his vile world of death and destruction. Over the top of her head, Logan scanned the body for anything that might identify the man. His eyes lighted on a custom-made ring on the fourth finger of the right hand. He took in the man's thin form, the once pristine, expensive suit and the dark-gold hair.

His mouth thinned into a hard, tight line. No, it wasn't his friend. The hair color, the elegant suit and the presence of the one-of-a-kind ring, all added up to one person—Jamie's partner, Hank Kessler.

The man's death raised some very interesting questions. If Jamie had discovered a deadly leak in Control, had he involved his partner in his covert investigation? Had Kessler been killed as a warning? Or had Kessler discovered that Jamie was the leak?

That last thought, which had only been a shadowy possibility last night, had suddenly turned into a very real probability. Logan knew very little. Garibaldi had told him that Jamie had some information about a possible traitor inside Control, that covert department he had been assigned to for the last six years. His boss had sent him to that meeting with Jamie last night that had turned out to be a trap. Now Kessler was dead, killed sometime last night and his body placed in Jamie's apartment. Why?

"He's dead." Emily's flat, bleak statement broke into his thoughts.

"Yeah, he is."

"Is he...was he...your friend?"

"My friend?" he echoed softly. "Yeah, I suppose you could say he was."

Logan tightened his hold on her, waiting for the reaction he knew would come once the shock had worn off. It didn't come. He knew they didn't have the time to wait around for it any longer.

Carefully, he set Emily aside, making sure she faced away from him, before he bent to perform the grisly but necessary task of searching the body. He found the wallet where he had expected to, and one brief look at the name on the driver's license confirmed his initial identification.

He returned the wallet to the inside pocket of the jacket. "Come on, let's get out of here."

"Out of here," she repeated dully. "We can't leave. That man's dead."

Rising, he dropped his hands over her shoulders. "Yes, he is. There's nothing we can do for him now."

He wasn't at all prepared for her to wrench herself away from his hands. Or for the heated defiance that snapped out of her eyes.

"A man's been murdered. We have to call the police."

He blinked, wondering if he had possibly lost his mind. No, he mused, she had lost hers. "Listen, honey—"

"My name," she cut in sharply, "is Emily."

Logan could only stare. He had been braced for tears, perhaps even open hysteria. He could even have handled it if she had fainted.

Despite the gruesome circumstance, despite the fact that they were embroiled in a dangerous, deadly situation, Logan laughed softly. There was much to admire about this woman. The information in her dossier had painted a very misleading picture. Beneath that tentative, timid exterior, beat the heart of a tigress.

That soft, amused chuckle grated on Emily's nerves. A small, insistent voice chided her for openly confronting this man. It was at war with another part of her that was horrified by the thought of just walking away, of leaving that poor soul lying on the floor.

"Well, are you going to phone the police?"

Logan's humor faded in an instant. "I can't."

"Why not?"

"Have you forgotten that you're not exactly here by choice? That I forcibly dragged you away from your home, your vacation, your life?"

Emily lowered her head, vividly recalling how she had gotten there. Perhaps she had forgotten, had blocked the whole thing from her mind. Maybe she had needed to forget.

What in the world was she doing? She was just an average person. She wasn't anything like the fictional characters she so admired, who could gracefully handle anything that was thrown their way. She wasn't gorgeous, or witty, or particularly interesting. She couldn't handle this.

She once again caught sight of that hand lying on the carpet. Emily made no effort to stop the shudder that ripped through her. "What are we going to do?"

"Leave."

"We just can't leave him like this."

"Why not? He's not going anywhere." He ran a hand through the slicked-back hair, ruffling it. "You're just going to have to forget about those rules your preacher of a father taught you. They don't apply not any longer. Not if we both want to survive."

It would be so easy just to believe that this man was really as cold and callous as he pretended to be. It would be so simple if she could look into the depths of those black eyes and ignore the compassion, the remorse and the understanding he tried so hard to hide.

This man had held her, had comforted her, had soothed her when she had been in shock. Not exactly an act of a desperate, hardened criminal. Something told her that he wouldn't just walk away—not if she asked him not to.

She lifted solemn eyes to him. "Because it's not right."

Damn! Damn! Damn! Logan knew he was lost. It went against his better judgment. It made a mockery of all the things he had learned about survival. Yet he knew that he was going to do it. For Emily.

"I'll call the police," he agreed wearily. "Anonymously. After we're far away from here and safe."

Leaving the Scaffers' home and coming to the control center in the basement of the safe house, only partially eased the thin man's anxiety. He couldn't afford to be connected to this affair. Not in any way. Not after he had taken such pains to remove himself from the picture.

Staring blankly at the gray walls, he knew he would feel better if someone, anyone had at least a clue to where Ghostrider had gone. Every hour the man remained on the loose made it all the more imperative to find him.

The phone on the table began to ring, and the thin man pounced on it.

"Corwin here. Just wanted to let you know that an unidentified couple just went into O'Connel's apartment house."

"A couple?" The thin man nearly choked on the sour taste of disappointment.

"Yeah, you did say you wanted to know about everyone who didn't belong in the building, didn't you?"

"Yes, I did," the thin man replied tersely. "Description?"

"Tall, dark guy in a flowered shirt. The broad's a blonde."

The pale eyes widened. What an interesting coincidence. It sounded like the same pair that Unit Three had spotted in the area of the Scaffers' house.

The thin man wasn't a big believer in coincidences. "Would you be able to identify them if you saw them again?"

"Sure thing. That guy's shirt was loud enough to give anyone a headache. And the blonde, well no guy is going to forget her in a hurry. Great legs."

The thin man's hand tightened on the receiver as he fought down the urge to crow in triumph. He had done it. Despite Zeus's cynicism and lack of confidence in him, he had done it. He had finally cornered the infamous Ghostrider.

A cruel smile spread over his mouth. "It's Logan," he snapped into the phone. "You know what you have to do."

After quietly slipping out of the service entrance of the apartment complex, Logan drove around for hours before he finally found a place in Apache Junction that suited him. A family-style motel that boasted rooms with better furniture and brighter colors than the apartment they had left. At least there was a print of the Superstition Mountains hanging on the wall to lighten the atmosphere.

And there was no dead body next to the bed.

This time, Emily didn't so much as blink an eye at the memory. In the past few hours, she had been pushed too hard, had felt too much terror, had seen too much. There was nothing left but a blessed numbness, and an urge to lie down on the king-size bed and sleep for a month. Straight.

The minute they had stepped into the motel room, Logan had taken up his favorite position by the room's only window. She didn't understand how he was able to stay on his feet. He hadn't gotten nearly the sleep she had last night, nor had she been up for thirty-six hours before that. Yet she was utterly exhausted.

It was satisfying that she had been right about Logan. From a pay phone outside a convenience store in Chandler, he had placed a call to the police to inform them about the body.

Emily sank onto the bed and let her head drop as her hands dangled between her thighs. He hadn't wanted to do it. Yet he had gone ahead and done it, because she had asked him to.

Everything about this dark, enigmatic man just didn't quite add up. Who was this man who called himself Logan? What had made him run?

Emily knew that her fear of him was slowly eroding. It had been awful when he had forcibly handcuffed her to the bed. Yet she couldn't help but recall his soft caress, the attempt to reassure her afterward. He had hauled her around the city against her will, yet he had offered his strength, his comfort, when she had needed it the most.

He hadn't hurt her. Not when she had tried to incapacitate him with a sharp knee to his most vulnerable place. Nor when she had made that panicked, futile bid for escape.

Emily passed a hand over her eyes. Maybe she was just rationalizing things. Maybe she just needed to believe there was more to Logan than he was showing. Maybe she was just slowly losing her grip on reality.

And maybe, she reflected wryly, she was feeling more than a bit guilty over that kiss they had shared this afternoon. And her reaction to it.

Nothing in her life had ever prepared her for this. Neither being abducted—nor being kissed senseless. Emily sincerely wished that she could be stronger, be able to stand toe to toe with Logan—despite her fears. Only she wasn't. She was just plain Emily Osborn, a seller of books, a dreamer of impossible dreams.

Maybe she should, as Logan had suggested, forget everything her father had taught her. Noah Osborn's rules wouldn't help her get through this. Her father...

Emily's eyes widened as she remembered Logan's exact words. Suspicion darkened them. "Mr. Logan?"

"What?"

"How did you know my father was a minister?"

He half turned from the window. "Your neighbor. She said he was a man of God. That translates into preacher in my book. He is, isn't he?"

"Yes." She paused. "I take it that apartment wasn't yours?"

"No, it belongs to another friend."

"Do you have a place in the city?"

"I don't really have a place anywhere." Briefly, Logan thought about the one refuge he had in the world. A beautiful little cabin tucked deep in the woods. The one place he could go where even Garibaldi couldn't find him. Only it wasn't home. It didn't even belong to him.

"Mr. Logan?"

A half-weary, half-cynical smile curved his mouth. "It's not mister anything. It's just plain Logan."

"Oh." Emily nervously licked her lips. "Is that your first name or your last?"

"Last."

"Can you tell me your first name?"

Gravely he studied her, and for a moment Emily thought he might not answer. "Trace. When I was born, my mother said there was a little trace of devil in me." He lifted a shoulder, a cloud passing over his expression, an unwanted memory. "I guess the name stuck."

"Your mother... is she still living?"

Fascinated, she watched as a muscle jumped in his jaw. It was somewhat reassuring to know that this man could feel ill at ease. It made him less formidable. It made him seem more human.

He slid a hand into the pocket of his pants. "Yeah, my mother's still living. So is my father. I also have a brother." Something briefly passed over his face. Something that looked like a spasm of regret.

"Is your brother anything like you?"

Emily was confused by the amused, secretive smile that softened his features.

"Just like me."

It was hard to imagine him with a family. He seemed so self-contained, so isolated, so...utterly alone. She couldn't begin to imagine anyone being "just like" Logan. "Where does your family live?"

He pinned her with an angry look. "Why all of the questions?"

That was rather obvious, Emily thought darkly. There was so much she needed to know. Why did he try so hard to hide the gentleness, the sensitivity, the softness? Why did he cover it up behind a ruthless, callous mask? How had he learned to handle everything they had been through in the past twenty-four hours? Who was Trace Logan, and could she really trust him?

One look at his hard expression and all her questions dried up. "I guess I want to know what's going to happen to me? I need to know if I can trust you."

He gave her a measured look. "I need to think on it. Why don't you try to get some sleep? After the day you've put in, you probably need it."

She didn't want to sleep. What she wanted was some answers. Only she didn't think she was going to get them.

Kicking off her sneakers, she lay down on the bed and pulled the light covers over her. Rolling into a tight ball, Emily wondered if she would ever manage to turn off the disturbing thoughts whirling around her head—enough to be able to sleep. For some inexplicable reason, she got the feeling that Logan didn't want her to trust him. Which was very odd, very confusing.

Then again, the whole day had been so confusing, so frightening. Worse, she had little idea what tomorrow would bring. Probably, she thought sleepily, it would bring more of the same.

Despite her troubled thoughts, Emily felt her body melt into the hard mattress as she drifted toward sleep.

"Emily?"

"What?" she answered drowsily.

"I'll try to make all of this end for you. I'll try to make sure that you're safe."

A sleepy smile curved her lips. For an abductor, Logan really was a nice man. He may believe that he didn't want her to trust him, but his actions, his words said differently. Suddenly, she found herself wanting to trust this man—needing to.

"Okay," she murmured.

"Emily?"

"Hmm."

"I'm sorry."

Emily snuggled closer to the pillow and let sleep finally overtake her as Logan's apology echoed in her mind.

Logan's head snapped away from the wall. He wasn't at all sure what had jerked him out of the light doze. He only knew that something didn't feel right.

Quickly, he scanned the quiet parking lot, on alert for the smallest detail, for anything that was out of place. He couldn't see a thing that hadn't been there an hour ago when he had laid his head against the wall to get some rest.

Yet his survival instincts were buzzing. Something didn't feel right. Then things hadn't felt right since he had accepted that last assignment in Panama.

Logan rubbed at the back of his neck. That had turned out to be a world-class fiasco. Not only had he stupidly blown the job as well as his cover, he had nearly bought the farm. At the time, he had little idea how it had happened.

It had only been when his boss, Garibaldi, had re-called him back in country and had briefed him on the things going on in Control that he began to have an ink-ling of what had gone wrong.

He knew that he hadn't blown the last assignment. He had been burned. Somebody had wanted him dead.

It had made him extremely cautious when he had ap-proached the Scaffer house. He had gone there early to check out the place, seen that the streetlights were out, seen that there were a lot of cars parked on the street in an area that had two-car garages and empty driveways.

Then he had spotted the men who were watching the Scaffers' house—who shouldn't have been there.

It hadn't felt right, so he had retreated to Emily's empty house to keep an eye on the street, and to watch for Jamie to warn him.

Now he felt stuck between the frying pan and the fire. He couldn't exactly trust Garibaldi since his boss had been the one who had sent him into that trap. He hadn't found Jamie, and had little idea if he could trust his former partner if he did find him. Another agent was dead, shot by an unidentified assailant for unknown reasons.

Logan rubbed at the knot of tension that had settled in the back of his neck. Garibaldi had informed him of a possible traitor in the department. A man who had been systematically leaking vital information over the past three years to an outside agent known only by the code name "Zeus." The result had been that three top agents, three good men, had been killed. After the disaster in Panama, the logical conclusion was that he was next on the list.

The problem, he grimly decided as his gaze swept over the parking lot, lay in figuring out who was behind it.

Was it Garibaldi himself, the head of the entire department? Could it be Pennington, the agent who was the liaison between Control and the various other intelligence branches?

Either of them had access to the kind of information that would be needed to take out those other three agents, and himself. Only four people positively knew of Ghostrider's existence. Only two of those people knew the whole story behind Trace Logan. Of the four, one of them was dead, another was missing, and the remaining two were the top people who ran Control.

Logan ignored the sharp pain that sliced through him. He didn't want it to be Jamie, the man who had been his partner, his mentor when he had first been recruited into the business. The only man who had been sent in to back him up when he had gone into deep cover. The man with the flaming red hair, the hard, craggy face and the soft lilting accent, who was closer to Logan than Tyler, his own brother.

It couldn't be Jamie. But from bitter experience, Logan knew that it was a possibility.

Hearing a soft, sleepy sound, Logan looked over at the double bed. The major regret he had over this whole affair was that he had been forced to drag this woman into this mess.

His expression softened as he continued to gaze at her. He envied Emily's ability to sleep so deeply, to have her rest undisturbed by feelings of punishing guilt or intense regret. Then, Logan thought wearily, she had no reason to be haunted by nightmares. She probably hadn't done anything in her life that wasn't morally right.

Innocent. Logan's eyes widened as he suddenly realized why he was so attracted to Emily Osborn. He had looked deeply into those wide, unprotected eyes and found her to be unspoiled, untouched by the darker side of life.

Not that she hadn't seen her share of the unpleasant realities of the world, Logan decided. Just that she seemed so unsullied by them, so full of trust. Emily seemed to be one of those people who believed that justice, that right not might, would win out in the end. She was like a bright beacon shining through the darkness in his soul, filling the shadow that had become his life with light.

It made him remember what he had been like ten years ago, so optimistic, so cocksure that there was truth and honor in the world. That he could, as his parents had taught him, make a difference. It made him want to believe that if he tried hard enough, believed in something strongly enough and worked long enough, he really could move mountains.

Only after living so long in the darkness, seeing the ugly underbelly of life, did Logan know that it was all a trick, a lie. Just as he knew that he couldn't use this woman and her innocence to heal all the scars that were etched into his soul.

He was smarter, stronger than that. He still had a few scruples left. The best thing he could do—the only thing—would be to get her as far away as possible from this situation. And from himself. Otherwise, his principles might not be able to hold out against his need for this woman and her innate gentleness.

Logan shook his head and froze when he caught the tiniest movement out of the corner of his eye. It was a tense few minutes for him, knowing something was out there, not being able to determine what it was.

Suddenly, he caught sight of another movement and his whole body went on alert. He had no way of knowing if it was just some petty thief who believed that the cars in the lot, the rooms in this motel, might provide him with some easy pickings. Or if somehow, someone had managed to track them to this place.

He couldn't take a chance. It didn't really matter who was out there. Logan knew he would have to get Emily out of there. And fast.

Quietly, he crawled over to the bed, hating the fact that he would have to wake this woman up and drag her out of bed. Grimly, Logan banished those soft thoughts.

Her dreams were filled with vaguely frightening images, shadowy figures. Emily ran through the mist, not knowing where to go, where to turn. Just as she stumbled and nearly cried out, she felt a rough hand coming over her face, blocking her breathing.

It's a dream, Emily tried to tell herself. Only it wasn't. Jerked awake, she vainly struggled against the hand covering her mouth, against the crushing weight that covered her.

"It's me. Logan." Instantly, she recognized the low voice, and stilled. "We've got company, the uninvited kind."

Harsh whispered orders were barked, and Emily instantly obeyed. Slipping out of the bed, she put on the tennis shoes Logan had made her wear, even though they had not quite jibed with the outrageous outfit he had picked out for her.

"Stay down."

Huddled up against the bed, she watched as Logan inched his way toward the bathroom. She started to follow, only to freeze when she heard the knob on the door slowly turning. Opening her mouth to warn Logan, Emily snapped it shut when she realized that he had already heard the giveaway sound. Only it was far too late as the door burst open to admit an ominous shadow.

Lightning fast, Logan pounced, kicking an object out of the figure's hand. A handgun landed over on the floor by the window, and she quickly scrambled over to retrieve it. Holding it unsteadily in both hands, she knew it was useless to her; she had no idea how to use it. It was a small consolation, knowing that while the gun was in her possession, the man who had burst into their room couldn't use it.

Helplessly, Emily watched as the two figures grappled on the floor. She cringed at the sound of flesh striking flesh, at the tense animal grunts. It passed through her mind that she needed to do something to help Logan. She didn't know what. It also occurred to her that this man might be a policeman, come to rescue her.

Emily dismissed that notion at once. This intruder was not a policeman. They didn't go creeping around in the night, breaking into motel rooms. They weren't, as far as she knew, even aware of her or her predicament.

Before she could decide on a course of action, Emily caught sight of another shadow sneaking through the open door. She spied the gun first as it poked in, aimed at the wrestling figures on the floor.

There was no time to think, only to act. Emily thrust out her leg several inches above the floor—directly in front of the figure. He tripped over the obstacle and went flying into the room with a startled cry.

"Run, Emily," she heard Logan's desperate command. Hopping to her feet, she hovered in front of the door in indecision. Without giving a thought to her own safety, she leaped onto the back of the second figure.

She was so determined, so terrified, that she didn't even realize that the body under her was motionless. Her only goal had been to prevent the second man from entering the fray, increasing the odds against Logan. Her head jerked up when she could no longer hear the sounds of the fight.

Hands settled on her shoulders, and Emily blindly struck out. "Lord, Emily," she heard Logan grunt as her fist struck the side of his jaw. "Come on, he's not going anywhere."

In horror, Emily scrambled off the man when it hit her that he wasn't moving, hadn't moved since he had flown into the room and hit the floor.

"Dear God, I've killed him."

Logan bent over and placed two fingers on the man's neck. "Out cold. He must have hit the dresser when he tripped."

He pulled a shaking Emily to her feet. "Come on, we've got to get out of here." Unceremoniously, Logan shoved her out the door.

Bent almost in half, Emily followed him, dodging through the parked cars. He was quicker, had the engine going, before she opened the door to the Rabbit and fell inside. He rammed the gearshift into reverse, had the car almost out of the parking lot, before she was able to shut the door.

Logan made for the highway at a terrifying rate, and Emily held her breath.

"Damn," she heard him swear softly. "I lost my gun."

Looking down, Emily saw that she was still clutching the gun she had retrieved, was amazed she had been able to hold on to it. "Here, have this one," she said, tossing the gun.

It landed square in Logan's lap. "Careful. You just about put me out of commission."

Furiously, she blushed, averting her head. Adrenaline was racing through her blood, and she was scared, confused and thoroughly upset.

So much so, it didn't hit her until Logan guided the Rabbit onto a dirt road that she'd had the perfect opportunity to escape during the confusion back at the motel. She could have run the other way when Logan had pushed her out the door. Not once had it crossed her mind to desert him.

Chapter 5

Logan scrubbed at his eyes, trying to relieve the dry grittiness that threatened to blur his vision. They had been on the road for hours. Since those men had found them at the motel, he had ditched the Rabbit and had stolen a pickup, then he had taken every deserted back road he could find, with no particular destination in mind. He was running—pure and simple.

The sun slipped over the horizon staining the barren, rocky landscape the color of blood. His mouth pulled down into a frown. It could have been his blood that had been shed last night. Or Emily's.

How in the sweet hell had those men found them? He ran a frustrated hand through his hair. He knew they hadn't been followed from Emily's house, or from Jamie's apartment. He had made damn sure of that.

His fingers clenched around the wheel. In spite of his precautions, their disguises, they must have been spotted at Jamie's place. They wouldn't have wanted to take him out in such a public place, not with so many witnesses around—not when they didn't know who the woman with him was. It would have been simple to slip a tracking device in the Rabbit while they had been inside. It would have completely eliminated the need to shadow them.

It had been a mistake, Logan berated himself, not to have switched cars after they had left Jamie's apartment. He hadn't wanted to upset Emily by the methods he would have to use. He hadn't wanted her to think he had lied to her, hadn't wanted her to think he was a criminal.

Yet she hadn't said a word when he had stolen the pick-up. She had pressed those dainty lips together, had given him a quelling look. He hadn't even gotten that when he had stopped to switch plates with a similar model.

Logan choked back a harsh, humorless laugh. He couldn't remember the last time he had actually cared what another person thought of him. In the past, the more frightened and terrified people were of him, the better his chances of staying alive.

Until now, he had been so intent on getting Emily safely away from those men, he hadn't spared a thought to how they had found them at the motel. How could he have let a little slip of a woman influence him into forgetting all the harsh lessons he had learned?

Logan cast a quick glance over at the silent woman, instantly feeling a flicker of remorse. It wasn't hard to see how the effects of exhaustion and fear had ravaged the delicate features. Now that the adrenaline had worn off, now that she'd had time to think, she no longer looked like a vulnerable, desert mouse. Emily Osborn looked like a woman who had been pushed to her limits—and beyond.

Why had he involved her in this mess? That wonderful innocence was slowly being ripped from her. He had crudely introduced her to his shadowy world of terror and deceit, destroying, he feared, something unique and precious. Her trust.

He had taught her the real meaning of fear. He had shown her how easily her own safe, predictable life could be so drastically altered by a quirk of fate.

Disgusted with himself, Logan felt compelled to ask, "How are you doing?"

"Okay." It was a dull, lifeless answer. It made him want to apologize. It made him long to promise that this nightmare was almost over.

Only he knew he couldn't. It was far from over. He wouldn't even be able to let her go now. They had been seen by those men in the white van in Emily's neighborhood just as they had been seen by those other two watching Jamie's apartment house. They would put it together and discover who was missing from her neighborhood. A couple of quick phone calls and they would find that Emily hadn't made her flight or arrived at her destination.

Since they had no idea he had kidnapped her, they would assume she was helping him. Her life wouldn't be worth spit if they ever got their hands on her. They would use her, drag information about him out of her. Then when her usefulness was over, they'd eliminate her.

"Who were those men back there?"

"They were the reason I was hiding in your house," he hedged.

"They weren't the police."

Logan was amazed by the dead certainty in her voice. "No, they weren't."

"Then why did they break into the motel? Why are they after you? How did they find us?"

"I think they planted a tracking device in the Rabbit." His lips tightened. "I found a bug in the phone at the apartment, which probably means the rest of the place was covered. We were made as soon as we stepped into the door."

Bugs? Tracking device? Emily shuddered. He had confirmed that those two men hadn't been the police, yet he had neatly avoided telling her who they really were. What had this man gotten himself into? What was she into?

She felt terribly confused, by her own actions, by his. What on earth had possessed her last night? Why hadn't she run when she had had the chance? Why had she so blithely turned over the gun? Had she lost every scrap of good sense she had ever had?

Emily hadn't acted, she was sure, out of fear. Otherwise she wouldn't have tried to help him when those two had burst into their room.

She sneaked a peek at the man driving the unfamiliar truck, and she knew she had acted the way she had because of Logan. Somewhere deep inside, in spite of his actions, in spite of her fear, she trusted him.

It didn't make any sense. "I can't believe I didn't run last night when I had the chance," she moaned.

Making sure to keep one eye on the road, Logan watched as several conflicting emotions passed over Emily's unguarded expression. He knew he should have never tried to reassure her, never let her see that he was anymore than what he appeared to be—a desperate man holding her against her will.

Logan knew better. He knew how risky, how dangerous it was to offer promises. By never offering them,
they could never be broken.

"Because somehow you must have realized you'd get
no help from those two." He gave her a tired, cynical
smile. "Better to stick with the devil you know than to
take on the ones you don't."

He caught the look of surprise on her face, of confusion. "Emily?"

"What?"

Logan heard the exhaustion in her voice. Heard
something that was even worse—resignation. "Why
don't you try to get some sleep?"

Dully she obeyed, tipping her head back against the
seat and closing her eyes. Logan felt the sharp blade of
guilt twist inside of him. Reaching over, he pulled her
down on the bench seat of the pickup, laying her head on
his thigh.

Looking down at the pale, colorless face, he felt a
feeling of intense tenderness and fierce protectiveness
flood through him. It had been so long since he had felt
even a hint of those two emotions.

There were people in his life he had cared about
deeply. There was his brother, Tyler, a man more dear to
him than his right arm. And there had been a time when
he would have unquestioningly laid down his life for
Jamie.

Never had he felt such a fierce, inexplicable need to
keep someone safe and unaware of the shadows and ugliness that hung over his life.

He wanted to now. For this delicate unspoiled woman
with the trusting eyes. He would see her through this
ordeal, unharmed and unsullied—before he quietly
slipped out of her life.

* * *

The thin man swore and jerked at his tie, unconcerned about his less than immaculate appearance. "What do you mean you lost them? They were sitting ducks in that motel. That's why I had you wait before taking them out."

He listened impatiently to the story being poured out on the other end of the line.

"We did manage to find the Rabbit, but he was already gone. But after that nothing. Zilch. It's like he disappeared into thin air."

"Naturally," the thin man quipped sarcastically. "Why do you think they call him Ghostrider?"

Only he knew better. Nobody was that good. Hadn't Logan messed up his last assignment in Panama? Because he was getting too old for this business. Isn't that why Garibaldi had jerked him back home? Because Logan was burned out and was losing it.

Logan wouldn't know a thing about this situation if it hadn't been for O'Connel. A stupid plan that could be laid right at Zeus's doorstep. If Zeus hadn't gotten so smug, hadn't considered himself immortal, invincible, none of this would have happened, and the thin man wouldn't have the thankless job of damage control.

He removed his reading glasses and pinched the bridge of his nose. He knew he had to find Logan, before this whole thing really got out of hand.

One fist came crashing down on the table. If only he had been willing to change the first plan, he could have had Logan and the woman picked up at O'Connel's place. If he'd decided to call the police when Logan was there and . . .

Suddenly a broad smile broke on his face. It was a brilliant inspiration, he decided. Ghostrider had made a mistake losing his gun at the motel. Now all the thin man had to do was to figure out how to use that mistake most effectively.

Logan scanned the area one more time before he entered the motel room. A quick glance at the bed revealed that Emily was still sleeping peacefully—exactly as she had been when he had left her an hour ago.

He hadn't, Logan knew, really taken much of a chance leaving her alone in the motel room while he searched through the shops in Sedona. She had been dead on her feet, and he had been certain nothing short of an atomic blast would arouse her from her deep slumber.

Dumping the two plastic bags on the dresser, Logan made straight for the bathroom. Stripping off the borrowed clothes, he stepped into the shower, turned on the water and stood under the lukewarm spray. Rubbing the cheap bar of soap over his body, he wished he could wash away all of his guilt, his regrets, as easily as he could the sweat and dirt.

Only he knew it was impossible. Grime was only skindeep—the other was ingrained into his soul.

Dipping his head under the thin stream of water, he ran the soap over his hair. He had no idea what he was going to do about Emily. There was no way he could let her go, nor could he take her with him.

He rested his forehead against the cool tiles of the shower stall. He was so damn tired. He couldn't remember the last time he'd had a decent night's sleep. That surely had occurred sometime before this last assignment. His lips curled into a grim frown. He couldn't remember the last time he'd had a peaceful night's rest, devoid of the vague, distressing nightmares that haunted him. That hadn't happened in six years.

Reaching up, he snapped off the water. Later he would decide what he was going to do about Emily. Right now he needed some sleep. Not a whole lot, just a few hours, and maybe then he would be able to think straight. Maybe he could find a way out of this mess. For Emily, for himself.

Hastily, he dried himself and pulled on the boxer shorts Emily had given him at her house. Logan wearily made his way back into the other room. He almost smiled when he spied the figure lying on the bed.

Yes, later, he silently promised. Later he would find a way to get Emily out of this, to keep her safe from the nastiness that had touched her life. Pulling down the bedspread, he slipped between the sheets.

He heard a soft, sleepy protest and smiled. Poor Emily. All in all, she really had come through everything that had happened rather well.

Softly, Logan chuckled, thinking what a tigress she had become last night when that second man had stepped into the room. He didn't know how she had gotten the man to the ground, but he could clearly remember that flying leap she had made onto the man's back.

Turning his head, Logan looked at the woman beside him, and knew that he was going to give into temptation. Wrapping his arms around her, he snuggled her body alongside his and closed his eyes. For the first time in a very long time, he fell into a dreamless sleep.

Once again Emily woke up disoriented and confused. She let her eyes drift around the unfamiliar room, trying to remember where she was.

They were in a motel room in Sedona, she suddenly recalled. A mere hundred and twenty miles north of Phoenix. A two and a half hour drive that had taken them over eight hours.

Them. Emily's eyes popped wide open. Even with the fuzziness of sleep, how could she have forgotten Logan? Her whole body went rigid when she realized there was a warm weight across the middle of her stomach, a hard body pressed up against her back.

Probing at her memory, she could recall Logan stopping at this out-of-the-way motel nestled among the huge pines in Oak Creek Canyon, of him leaving her in the car unguarded while he went inside the office to get one of those cabins across the road from the rushing creek. If she probed a bit more, she could remember stumbling into the room intent on one thing only—the comfortable bed that dominated the pine-paneled room.

Easing out from under the weight of the arm and away from Logan, Emily was relieved to see she was still wearing the outlandish outfit Logan had picked out for her. The only thing she hadn't been too tired to remove were her sneakers.

Once she made it to the bathroom, Emily secured the lock and wearily slipped out of her wrinkled clothes. The water in the shower was barely warm. It didn't bother Emily. She was thoroughly grateful to be able to feel clean again.

Well, not completely clean, Emily thought with a sigh as she rinsed the thin lather off her body. There was no shampoo, so she couldn't wash her hair. She hadn't had, she realized, even a passing acquaintance with a toothbrush since yesterday morning.

Emily straightened as a wave of shock rippled through her. Had it only been yesterday when she had awakened to find herself handcuffed to her own bed? Had it been less than forty-eight hours since she had returned home—only to be assaulted by an intruder?

It had been, Emily realized with a start, a little over thirty-six hours since this whole ordeal had begun. It felt like a lifetime had passed.

Stepping out of the shower, Emily realized she felt better. She didn't want to put on the soiled clothes. There was little else she could do. She could hardly parade around in front of Logan inadequately dressed in the motel's towel.

Logan. The name rippled through her, making her feel instantly, uncomfortably aware. It struck her as strange that he hadn't awakened when she had slipped out of bed.

Quickly, she scrambled into her clothes. Quietly, she opened the bathroom door. Logan lay approximately where he had been when she had left him, on his side with his back to her, one arm flung out over the place she had vacated.

He was dead asleep. The perfect opportunity, she realized, for her to make an escape. Emily bit the inside of her cheek, wondering why the thought of ending the nightmare didn't fill her with relief. Whatever he was involved in, whoever he was running away from, it had nothing to do with her.

It struck her that even though she was thinking of escape, it hadn't crossed her mind to go to the authorities. She wouldn't go to the police. Not unless she thought they could help Logan.

Frowning, Emily stepped into the middle of the room, debating what she should do. Last night had changed things. Drastically. She was no longer just an unwilling piece of excess baggage to be disposed of at the first opportunity. By her own actions, she had turned into someone who had actually aided and abetted her own abductor. She had somehow stepped over the line from victim to accomplice. Willingly.

"You should have left while you had the chance." The lazy voice filled with dry humor made her head snap up. She didn't need to look into the hooded eyes to know that Logan was awake, that he had been for quite some time.

It was eerie how this man seemed able to discern her thoughts. She had never been good at lying, had no practice at subterfuge, yet she hadn't thought she was so transparent. Or maybe it was only with this man that she couldn't hide her thoughts.

Trying to salvage some of her pride, Emily lifted her chin. "I couldn't. You would have stopped me."

He laughed softly. "Yeah, I probably would have. Yet you didn't even try."

Hot color flooded her cheeks as Emily dipped her head. Just a few short hours ago she would have. And he knew it.

As he jumped from the bed, Emily could only stare at Logan's lean body clad only in a pair of her brother's boxer shorts. The bronze of his skin stood out sharply against the white material.

One hand came up to lift her chin. "I'm glad you didn't."

"Why?" she asked a bit breathlessly.

"Because you're a hell of a lot safer with me."

"Am I?"

That softness fled from his face, and Emily shivered. "Those men who broke into the room last night undoubtedly know who you are by now. They'll assume you're helping me."

"But how?" She saw his expression become closed, shuttered. "I know, I know," she muttered bitterly. "It's better if I don't know."

Those strong hands came up to cup her shoulders. Emily felt a shiver of feminine awareness, of excitement, race down her spine.

"I would tell you if I thought it wouldn't put you in more danger than you already are. But I can't. For your sake."

One tanned finger brushed lightly over her cheek. "I know it's a lot to ask but couldn't you just trust me?"

Trust me. Famous last words, Emily thought tartly. Yet that's exactly what she had done. She had trusted him. Twice now, she had let the opportunity to escape pass by. She hadn't trusted those men last night, had a feeling that they hadn't cared that she was an innocent victim of circumstance.

She had chosen to stick with the devil she knew. She had chosen to stay with Logan.

As she slowly nodded, a broad grin broke out over his face revealing white, even teeth. It caused Emily's breath to catch in her chest. He was so incredibly appealing, especially when he smiled. A real smile, without a trace of that habitual cynicism.

"That's good, Emily." His hands stroked lightly over her shoulders. "I promise you that just as soon as it's possible, this whole thing will be over for you."

Staring down at her trusting eyes, Logan deliberately ignored the warning bells going off in his head. This was one promise he knew he had to make, knew he had to keep.

The fresh scent of soap drifted to him, and Logan inhaled deeply. The soft satin of her warm, slightly moist skin, felt so soothing against his dry, hot palms. It came to Logan that he was still idly caressing Emily—long after her need for reassurance had passed.

Abruptly, he pulled his hands away, highly aware of the disturbing reaction of his body. Never in his life had such a simple thing, the soft scent of woman and the silken feel of feminine flesh, gotten such a swift, violent reaction. Quickly he turned, before Emily could become aware of the changes she had aroused in his body.

"I bought some things while you were sleeping." He pulled some articles out of the bag. "For disguises," he explained at Emily's blank expression.

In amazement, Emily looked over the odd assortment of things Logan placed on the dresser. There were various packages of makeup and two boxes of hair dye. From another sack, he pulled out some clothes.

"You want me to dye my hair," Emily burst out in astonishment.

"Yeah. It's not only cooler than a wig, it's safer. There's less chance to lose it that way." He pulled out another item from the bag. "I also want to cut it."

Her astonishment quickly turned into horror as her hands flew to her hair. "You want me to cut my hair?"

Logan's expression softened. "It'll be easier to dye."

"Except for an occasional trim, I've never let anyone cut my hair. Not even my mother when she decided it was time to cut it to a respectable length."

The image of this desert mouse rebelling against her mother brought a smile to Logan's lips. "Why is it so important that you not cut your hair?"

A blush blossomed on her pale cheeks. "I always thought that my hair was my best features." She shook her head, folding her hands together in a prim gesture. "I guess that's why my mother wanted it cut. Pride goeth before a fall."

Logan was startled by her reply. She acted as if her hair was the only good quality she possessed. Didn't she realize that those warm blue eyes could make a man long to move mountains for her? Wasn't she aware that she had a pair of legs that could make a grown man drool?

Apparently not. The knuckles he brushed over her silky cheek were warmed by the blush that hadn't faded. "It'll be okay. I promise you."

It didn't feel okay. Emily sat stiffly on the edge of the chair, closing her eyes when the first long strands fell into her lap. The sound of the scissors slicing through her hair made her cringe.

It felt as if hours had passed before Logan finally finished. "It's not bad, not bad at all."

Lifting her from the chair, he positioned her in front of the mirror hanging over the dresser. It took her several moments to work up the courage to open her eyes.

It was awful. It was all gone, the long golden hair she had secretly taken such pride in. She felt light-headed, missed the weight, the way her hair had brushed against the back of her neck and shoulders.

Emily felt a tear escape to slip down her cheek. Other tears quickly followed.

Logan felt terrible. She hadn't cried when she'd thought he was a criminal who would hurt her. She had borne the shock of discovering a dead body. She hadn't lost her head when she'd thought she had killed a man.

To see her mourn the loss of her hair hurt. He gathered her into his arms.

"It'll grow back," he promised. "I wouldn't have done it if it hadn't been necessary."

"But it's so ugly."

"Ugly?" Logan nearly laughed out loud. Tipping her head, he used a thumb to dry her cheek. "Oh honey, you couldn't be ugly if you tried."

He could see she didn't believe him. There was one way he knew to convince her that she was still a lovely, desirable woman.

Slowly, he rubbed his mouth over hers, felt a tiny resistance in her lips. They softened, fell open with a mute invitation when he used the tip of his tongue to moisten her lips.

This time she needed no prompting as her arms slipped around his waist and snuggled closer into his embrace. Logan nearly lost it. He knew he was treading a fine line, knew how little it would take for him to fall right over the edge.

Yet he knew he had to touch her—just once. Sliding a hand under the thin top, he cupped a breast. She was small, but so sweet. When he heard her low gasp, he knew he was perilously close to finding out just how sweet she was.

He wanted to slowly peel off her clothes and taste every warm inch of her. He wanted to lay her down on the bed and find out how it would feel to have those gorgeous legs wrap around him.

Only he couldn't. He had promised to keep her safe— not to seduce her. From her eager response, he realized just how easy that would be.

Easing away from her, Logan dropped his hands, amazed at how unsteady they were. He couldn't remember any woman who could make him tremble. He couldn't recall ever wanting another woman this badly. He had to remind himself that this was a woman he could never have.

* * *

Emily could only gape at the unfamiliar redhead that stared back at her from the motel mirror. The newly shorn hair, the different color and the bold, striking clothes Logan had purchased, made her look so different. Running a hand down the expensive sundress she wore, she would have never thought that a redhead would be able to wear such diverse shades of lavender.

She studied herself in the mirror. The flame color of her hair brought out an almost delicate shade of pearl in her skin, made her too-light eyes a darker, more interesting shade of blue. The rich color helped disguise the less than professional cut.

Maybe it wasn't so bad. She sneaked a shy peek at Logan in the mirror. A new, but definitely not improved Logan. She had cut his hair at his request, and he had applied some dye, turning those gorgeous blue-black locks into a dull brown. He had kept Luke's white pants, yet had topped them with an ugly shirt in a tasteless shade of pea green.

Somehow he had acquired a pair of glasses, and there was a new, definite slouch to his straight, proud walk. He looked like a vacationing accountant from Debuque—average, middle class, totally unremarkable. He looked nothing like the man who had held her—had kissed her like she was the most beautiful woman in the world.

She saw a quick frown darken his face as he caught sight of her studying him in the mirror. "Is something wrong?" she asked.

Logan didn't immediately answer. The image he had painstakingly created for her was absolutely perfect. It would focus people's attention squarely on Emily—instead of on him. They were looking for a colorless blonde who appeared timid, a woman who would very likely bolt if someone said boo. They wouldn't think a thing about a well-turned-out redhead who looked hot, hungry and ready for action.

Everything about her now felt wrong, jarred on his senses. It surprised Logan that he preferred Emily the mouse over Emily the wanton.

"Nothing," he finally managed to mumble. "I'm a bit worried because we're low on cash. I used quite a bit for the motel rooms, and the stuff I bought this morning."

"Well I have some—" Emily abruptly trailed off. The traveler's checks she'd gotten for her vacation were safely tucked inside her purse—back in Phoenix. "Nothing," she finished lamely. "Don't you have any credit cards, or even a bank card?"

He had a wallet full of cards, Logan mused. All of them under an assumed name, his latest identity since returning to the States.

They were all worthless. Anything he charged on them would be reported right back to Control. It would take someone with the use of a computer about five minutes to track his movements.

"I can't use them. I'd leave a paper trail any fool could follow."

As she bent her head to study the problem, it suddenly struck Emily that they were in Sedona, a mere stone's throw from Flagstaff. "We can get some money from my brother. Luke has a restaurant up in Flagstaff."

He waved a hand in the air. "Too dangerous."

"Why?"

"Because if those men know about you, you can be sure they know about your brother. You can bet they'll have people watching him, in case you show up."

"Oh, I didn't think..." There had to be a way. "Those men are looking for Luke's blond sister. They won't think twice about a redheaded girlfriend."

She could tell he was tempted. He didn't particularly like it, but he was tempted. Because he was desperate, she supposed.

"It's too damn dangerous."

"Is it because you don't trust me?" she returned slowly. "Because you think I'll give you away to Luke?"

Tension, thick and heavy, flowed into the room. Vigorously, he shook his head. "No, I trust you. I have to."

It wasn't quite the response Emily needed, but it was understandable. She too trusted Logan. She had to.

"Listen, I'm hungry. I think I've got enough cash left for a decent meal. How about we go out for a steak?"

Emily slowly nodded. "That would be lovely. I just need to freshen up first."

She fled into the bathroom feeling confused and elated. He must trust her. Otherwise they would go to a take-out place and bring the food back here to consume—where they wouldn't be seen. Steak hardly sounded like fast food.

Emily fiddled with her hair, unaccustomed to the short length. It was odd that he should know so much about makeup and clothes. He was extremely good at this disguise business. He had literally taken a few simple items and had used them to create an entirely different look for her, a new Emily.

She smiled wryly at the strange reflection in the mirror. A new look maybe, but still the same old Emily.

Giving her hair one final pat, she returned to the other room.

Logan had turned on the television, and the muted sound of the local evening news broadcast floated in the room. Just as she was about to let him know she was ready, something flashed on the screen that captured her attention.

Prominently displayed next to a fuzzy, indistinct picture of Logan was a photo of her taken from her college yearbook during her senior year. It was a dreadful picture, and Emily was aghast to see it on the screen.

Listening to the rapid, machine-gun-style delivery of the newscaster, she froze. The commentator said that Logan's name was Nick Foster and that he was wanted for questioning by the police. They were also looking for her, as a possible accessory to murder.

Chapter 6

Logan watched the newscast in growing disbelief. A muscle jumped in his jaw as both hands curled into tight fists. This was what happened when he ignored his instincts and training. By giving into Emily, he had laid himself wide open for attack. He should have known better than to try to be Mr. Nice Guy.

Now, they were being hunted. Whether by Control or the leak, it didn't matter. They were going to throw him to the wolves, or in this case, to the Arizona police.

It would never get that far, Logan knew. Someone, perhaps even Garibaldi himself, was going to use the police to find him. Not so he could take the fall for killing Kessler. Logan's mouth flattened into a grim line. He was being set up to be murdered.

There was no doubt of that in his mind. He had just been declared a rogue, an agent gone bad. By showing his picture, by revealing his current identity, they had made him an open target for the police—or for any other agent.

And Emily, as well.

Emily! Oh hell, Logan mentally swore, turning. He spotted her over by the bathroom door, white-faced, her fist jammed into her mouth to prevent herself from screaming. She was no longer looking at him with trusting eyes. There wasn't just fear in them. She was looking at him in horror.

"Emily?" He took a tentative step forward. She scrambled away from him.

"You lied to me."

Logan inwardly cringed at the shaky, desperate-sounding voice. She was riding along the fine, sharp edge of panic—ready to slide over.

"You told me your name was Logan. You told me you weren't a criminal."

"It is. I'm not," he returned flatly.

"But the police are looking for you, because of that man we found." What little color was left in her face instantly drained. "Good Lord, they're looking for me."

"It's a lie. A cleverly constructed one and very misleading. But it's still a lie." Logan held her eyes with his. "You should know that better than anyone."

Emily shook her head. "But they said . . ."

He'd had enough. Logan took another step only to have her dodge away from him. This time he didn't let her get away with it.

He feinted to the right, and when she tried to move in the opposite direction, he grasped her by the upper arms. There was a burning sensation in the pit of his stomach that he couldn't easily ignore. He couldn't bear to see this woman so frightened, so very close to losing control—all because of him.

"You know better than anyone else that I couldn't have possibly killed Kessler." He kept his voice low, soothing, commanding.

Wary eyes flickered over to the television. "But they said—"

"What they were told to say," he cut in sharply. "How could I have killed Kessler after midnight Sunday morning when I've been with you since Saturday night?"

Darkened lashes fluttered down over her eyes. Once. Twice. The panic lessened as rational thought began to take over. Carefully, he eased the pressure, turning the bruising grip into a soft, reassuring caress.

"Unless you believe I slipped out when you were asleep to do away with Kessler," he added quietly.

A thousand conflicting thoughts swirled inside Emily's head, along with too many questions that had no answers. There was only one thing Emily could hold on to. The knowledge that Logan, or rather Foster, or whoever he really was, had not left her house that night. What would have been the point? Why would he have returned, after he had gotten cleanly away? That wouldn't have made any sense. Then, hardly any of this made any sense, Emily thought wryly.

Logan hadn't killed that man. Of that, Emily was very sure. But that didn't answer any of the thousands of other questions that she had. She lifted her eyes. "Why did that newscaster say your name was Nick Foster?"

She heard him slowly let out a breath. It sounded like a sigh. Trembling, she kept her eyes on his, fighting against the mesmerizing quality of his black fathomless gaze.

"Because that's who my identification says I am."

Emily sneaked her tongue out to moisten her lips. She didn't like the sound of that. "Who are you really?"

"A good question." That sardonic half smile was again playing around the beautiful mouth. "Up until six years ago, I was mostly Trace Logan."

"Mostly?" she echoed blankly. "What exactly does that mean?"

"That it was necessary for me to use other identities."

It was sounding worse all the time. What kind of person found it necessary to be someone else for a while? Emily didn't care for any of the answers that were coming to mind. "What happened six years ago to make you stop being Trace Logan?"

"He died."

Emily felt as though she were slowly losing her mind. She had already realized that she had lost her grip on reality—ever since she had walked into her house and had been captured by a tall dark man with secrets in his eyes.

She jerked herself away from those soothing hands. It was ridiculous, insane, to feel such heat, such electricity at the touch of a man who was not at all what he seemed.

"You're not making any sense," she snapped.

"Six years ago, Trace Logan died in the crash of a small aircraft."

"He was? You mean . . . you were. . . ." She wanted to throw up her hands in confusion, in despair. "Do you have any idea how crazy that sounds?"

Logan shrugged. "It's quite simple really. The people I worked for needed a man without a traceable past. Without an identity. One with a clean slate, upon which they could write anything they chose."

He paused, a cynical smirk twisting his lips. "I became that man, Emily. My records were sealed, my very existence erased. I became a nonentity, a man with no name, no family, no past. A ghost if you will, able to be anything or anybody."

Emily shook her head in bafflement, in denial.

"I'm what is known in the trade as a spook," he went on with a touch of amusement. "I'm an agent in place. I work for the government, an intelligence branch."

In other words, he was a spy. Emily wanted to wipe that hateful smile off his mouth. He really must think she was crazy, or very gullible, to swallow that old tired line.

"How very original," she retorted tartly. "Isn't that the very same thing any criminal, conman or liar would trot out to justify such bizarre, questionable behavior?"

Instead of being affronted or indignant, he merely laughed. "It is rather overused."

Logan knew he shouldn't be telling her this. He had a dozen different stories on the tip of his tongue. He could drag out any one of them and, in a very short while, have Emily convinced he was telling the truth.

But at the very last minute he had found it was impossible to lie. Not to this woman. Through a twist of cruel fate, she had literally stumbled into his life, into a mess that she had no part in making. One he wasn't sure he was going to be able to fix.

Whoever was after him had made her, had thrown her to the wolves. Her life was in danger right along with his. At the very least, Emily deserved the truth.

"I was recruited just a month before my graduation. Like most twenty-three-year-olds, I was flattered, honored to be chosen." A cold smile touched his lips. "And cocky. My dad was a lifer in the marines, very big on honor, and doing service for one's country. I figured it was my duty to accept the privilege, the honor that was being bestowed on me.''

The smile dropped from his mouth. ''I've long since learned it wasn't a privilege, but a burden. The youthful arrogance has long been weeded out—along with the ideals.''

Her knees were no longer quite able to support her, so Emily sank down onto the edge of the bed. She didn't know what to believe. It wasn't what he'd said that had brought on this confusion. It was the bitterness, the deep pain she had detected in his voice that was at odds with the cold look in his eyes.

''You're really serious about this.''

''Most definitely. I've told so many stories, so many lies in the course of my job, there's a dozen different explanations I could give you. And it wouldn't take me very long to convince you—of any of them. But I won't,'' he added gravely. ''I may not be able to tell you certain things for your own protection, but I won't ever lie to you.''

Emily lowered her eyes and studied the hands that lay limply in her lap. She really must be crazy. She was beginning to believe him.

''That plane crash, it was faked, wasn't it?''

Logan stuffed his hands into his pockets and tipped a shoulder against the wall. ''Six years ago, my superior wanted to move me into a highly specialized unit known as Damage Control. We take on the nastiest, most hopeless situations in a last-ditch effort to salvage them. They needed men who could slip into a volatile situation without creating a ripple, and who could then slide out again without leaving a trace.''

"And they needed you," Emily supplied soberly.

"Yes."

"But what about your family? Did they know the plane crash was a fake?"

"No." That curtain that effectively veiled his eyes, parted for a moment, giving Emily a glimpse at the man's inner turmoil—and his regrets. "It was safer that way, for them, for me. My boss sealed my records, and I became Ghostrider. A man with no family, no past, no name."

"No name," she repeated softly. "Then why did you give it to me?"

He half turned from her. "After everything I had put you through, I guess it was the least you deserved."

Carefully, she turned his story around in her mind, probing for flaws. Something wasn't right.

"Why can't you just go to your agency and get them to help you?"

"I can't." He drew one hand out of his pocket to rake it through the dull brown hair. "By leaking my picture to the news, by revealing my current identity, the very one they supplied for me, the agency has declared me a rogue. An agent gone bad—out of control. Do you understand what I'm saying?"

No, Emily thought helplessly, not really. "Is that like on the spy show on television when that man says if any of your agents are caught or killed, the secretary will disavow any knowledge of their actions?"

He smiled softly at her reference. "I suppose it is, in a way." The smile instantly fell. "Somebody wants me out of the way. They want me dead."

How many more shocks could she withstand in such a short period of time? Perhaps, Emily reflected, she was becoming immune to them. She wasn't nearly as stunned or horrified as she thought she would be.

"By showing your picture along with mine, they are decreeing that you are to share the same fate as mine."

She wasn't quite as immune as she had thought. Emily started to tremble. "I've never had anyone want to kill me before," she whispered hoarsely. "No one has ever hated me that much. I've never been that important. Why would someone want me dead?"

"Because you can clear me of Kessler's murder. They don't want that."

"They? Who are *they,* Logan?"

"That I can't tell you." Swiftly, he leaned down and placed a gentle hand over her mouth. "Can't, Emily, not won't. I wasn't being arbitrary when I said it would be better for you if you didn't know all the details. If by any chance you should fall into the hands of those men from last night, or any others from Control, you can truthfully say you don't know a thing. With that innocent face and honest eyes, maybe you'll be believed. It just might save your life."

"Might?" She tried to swallow around the very large lump that had lodged in her throat. This was more of a nightmare than she had ever imagined, and it just kept getting worse.

Softly his thumb traced over her lower lip, parting it to rub lightly over the hard ridge of her teeth. "I wish I could offer you a guarantee. I wish I could promise you it will turn out right, but I can't. I won't. I haven't really lied to you before, and I won't start lying to you now."

It may be foolish, it may be gullible, Emily thought, but deep down, she believed every word he had told her, despite Logan's confession that he was an accomplished, convincing liar.

Looking straight into his eyes, Emily probed past the curtain he used so effectively to guard his secrets. No matter how hard Logan tried to portray himself as a cold, emotionless man, she knew differently. There were deep, volatile emotions swirling around inside this man that he worked hard to keep severely banked and cleverly hidden behind a mask of indifference. She had seen the pain when he had spoken of his family, she had felt his remorse.

He had also given her something that was quite precious. He had told her his name.

Twisting her hands together, Emily wondered just how many of her thoughts were true, or if it was all just wishful thinking. Perhaps she just wanted him to be a caring man. Perhaps she needed him to be.

In the end, Emily knew that she would have to rely on her instincts—and pray that they were right.

"What are we going to do now?"

Logan squatted down in front of her. Picking up both her hands, he laced his fingers through hers. "Having the police looking for us changes things. I don't really want to do it, but our options have suddenly become severely limited."

"Do what?"

"Go to your brother for some money. He'll give it to you, won't he?"

Emily nodded gravely. "He will if I ask. Luke's never been able to say no to anything I ask of him. He's always felt guilty because he was able to get away with so much when we were children, while I always was the obedient one."

Logan gently touched her cheek. "A typical preacher's kid. A real hell-raiser."

"No. Luke just wanted a normal childhood. He just wanted to be like all the other kids."

His fingers curled around her ear, threaded themselves through her hair. "And what did Emily want?"

"The same thing," she admitted in a barely audible voice. "Only I didn't have the courage to defy my parents."

One dark eyebrow rose in disbelief. "Sure you did. You stood up to your mother when she wanted to cut your hair. I'll just bet when it came to the important stuff, you stood your ground. You certainly didn't have any problem defying me."

"Well, I suppose." She ducked her head. "There was this missionary my parents wanted me to marry."

Something tightened in Logan's gut. Something ugly slid into his mind. If it didn't sound quite so insane, he would have sworn he was jealous of a man who had played such a prominent part in Emily's life.

"Did you love him?" It just slipped out, yet Logan waited for her answer.

"No. He didn't love me, either. Otherwise . . ."

"Otherwise what?" he coaxed.

That delightful, predictable blush stole into her cheeks. "Nothing. It doesn't matter."

Logan could see it did. He wanted to demand that she tell him.

"We can trust Luke," he heard Emily reassure.

Logan let it go—for now. He knew that someday he would find out what she had been too embarrassed, too shy to say. Someday soon. They were running out of time.

"Would you get a load of that!" The long, low wolf whistle emitted by his partner grated on Corwin's nerves.

Although it was the third time in less than an hour, his weary eyes automatically lifted to peer out of the windshield of the dark sedan.

Immediately, he spotted a woman walking on the sidewalk. Naturally it would be a redhead, he thought wearily. Hadley had a thing for redheads. Corwin preferred blondes.

After a quick but thorough appraisal, Corwin dismissed the woman in the lavender dress. She may have had a great pair of legs, but she was far too rich for his blood.

He was bored, Corwin decided. After that disastrous attempt at the motel, the chief had ordered them to this deadly boring stakeout as punishment for their failure to capture Ghostrider. Poor Hadley, Corwin thought with a snicker. His partner still sported a goose egg the size of a walnut on his forehead from that fiasco.

Corwin frowned. He sported a bruised ego for allowing Ghostrider to best him. The chief had been wrong. The guy may be getting up there, but he wasn't close to losing it. The man had been good. Damn good. And Corwin had the sore muscles and bruises to prove it.

"She's going into the restaurant," Hadley needlessly informed him.

With a long-suffering sigh, Corwin reached for the door handle.

"You going in?"

"Yeah, I'm going in. I gotta make sure the broad's only gonna get some lunch, and not meet with Osborn. You know the chief's orders."

"Yeah, the chief's orders," Hadley echoed in disgust.

Corwin suppressed a smile as he darted across the street. Poor Hadley. He may have lost to an experienced man, one reported to be the best in the business. Hadley had been taken down by a woman who could hardly weigh more than a hundred pounds soaking wet.

Well, at least this broad was a looker, Corwin thought as he pushed open the glass doors to the restaurant. With any luck at all, she would order something to eat, giving him a chance to have a cup of coffee served in a mug instead of a foam cup. At least he would be out of the stifling heat of the car for a while.

Emily nervously wiped her damp palms on the skirt of the sundress as her eyes adjusted to the dimness in the hall. This whole thing was more nerve-racking than she had anticipated. The simple three-block walk from where Logan had parked the car had been an ordeal. She had been in constant fear that someone might recognize her—despite her disguise.

According to what the pretty hostess had told her, at least her brother was in his office, and not out in the public part of the restaurant. Her hand hesitated when she reached for the knob. She hoped Luke would not ask too many questions or expect too many answers. She couldn't lie to him. She had never been good at lying and Luke would know if she tried. He always knew when she tried to keep anything from him.

Emily lifted her other hand to knock. It paused in midmotion. What if Luke had seen the news? If he had any suspicion that his sweet, law-abiding sister was wanted by the police in connection with a murder, he would never let her leave. Not without hearing the whole story first. Maybe not even then.

She would handle it, Emily sternly told herself. She could handle Luke. She had to.

With a brief knock on the door, she slipped inside Luke's office without waiting for a response. He was sitting behind his cluttered desk, his blond head bent as he studied some papers. The ever-present mug of coffee was by his hand. Emily checked the urge to make sure it was decaffeinated. With the amount of coffee he drank, she had long ago convinced him that caffeine was bad for him.

Briefly, he glanced up when she entered the office. "Sorry. If you're here about the waitress job, you'll have to come back this afternoon."

He hadn't recognized her! Her own brother hadn't known her!

"I'd make a terrible waitress, Luke, as you well know."

His head jerked up, causing a lock of spun-gold hair to fall over his tanned forehead. Navy blue eyes widened in surprise as that squared, firm jaw dropped open. It really wasn't fair, Emily thought wryly, for Luke not only to have inherited all the flair and style in the family but also to have gotten the lion's share of looks.

"Emily?" His jaw snapped closed. "What in the hell are you doing here?"

"Is that any way to greet our favorite sister?"

He leaped from the chair, and rushed to gather her into his arms. For one brief moment she clung to him, needing his strength, his solid warmth, his familiarity. Then knowing she had to, Emily pushed herself away.

"You are my *only* sister," her brother retorted tartly. "And you're supposed to be in Hawaii."

Emily smiled faintly at Luke's accusing tone. He was the one who had pushed her into taking a vacation, and yet had predicted that she never would.

A hand reached up to touch her hair. "What in the hell have you done to yourself?"

Emily bit the inside of her cheek. He obviously hadn't seen the news. She braced herself, not to lie, but to do a bit of fancy sidestepping. "You've been after me for years to change my image. Don't you like the new me?"

Keeping his hands on her arms, Luke stepped back as he pursed his lips into a thoughtful frown. His eyes traveled over her from the top of her head to the tips of her toes.

"As a man, my only comment would be..." He let out a very loud, very appreciative masculine whistle. "As your brother, I can only bemoan the fact that my business is going to suffer. It's going to go to hell while I'm busy trying to keep drooling men away from my very sexy sister."

"Oh, Luke." Emily laughed. She didn't believe a word of it. It was part of Luke's considerable charm, that ability to make any woman feel beautiful and special—even if that woman was only his sister.

He guided her over to a couch and sat down beside her, holding both of her hands between his much larger ones. "Okay, darlin', now give. What's this all about?"

"Do I need a reason to come see my brother?"

Luke ignored the question as he leaned back against the couch. "It has to be something big, important enough to drag you away from the store. I don't think you came all the way up here just to show me the new you."

Emily lowered her eyes. "I need a favor, Luke. I need to borrow some money."

She heard Luke swear softly and cringed, knowing how appalled her parents would be to know that their one and only son used that kind of language so easily, so casually.

"The last time I lent you something was back in seventy-six as I recall."

Emily nodded, feeling overwhelmed by a flood of warm memories. "Your favorite record album."

"You scratched it, and I distinctly remember your vowing never to borrow anything from me again."

Emily felt the heat rushing to her cheeks. She knew exactly what Luke was trying to do. Only she wasn't that scared little girl who needed prodding to pour out her troubles to her big brother.

No, she thought dryly, she was now a big, scared girl who was in way over her head.

His hand curled into a fist, and he slipped it under her chin to lift her face. "What gives, Em."

"I . . . I can't tell you. I just need you to loan me some money, without asking any questions."

Her brother's handsome face instantly clouded over, grew stern. "What makes you think that I'll just give you money, that I'll let you walk out the door without a word of explanation."

"You will."

"Why should I?"

"Because I'm asking you to."

Another oath escaped from him, and Emily held her breath, praying that what she had told Logan was the truth.

Luke had stood by her when she had broken off her engagement to Jacob Ridley. He had supported her decision to open up the bookstore when her parents had tried to talk her out of it.

She hoped he would support her now. If Luke decided to push it, Emily didn't know if she would be able to hold out against him.

"Okay, Em." She breathed a sigh of pure relief at the sound of defeat in Luke's voice. "I'll lend you the money, and I won't ask questions, only if you'll promise that you'll let me know if you need any more, if you need me."

She gave him a grateful smile. "I will. If I need anything, I'll send you a telegram using the code we made up when we were kids."

He was, Emily could see, straining against the need to ask why she would have to contact him using the childish, but effective code they had set up to fool their parents. He wouldn't push it. Because she had asked him not to.

Luke rose from the couch and walked over to the floor safe behind the desk. "How much?" Emily named a figure that she knew would have him raising his brows in astonishment.

"Here it is, plus a little more." He held up his hand to stop her protest. "Take it, and for God's sake, be careful. You really shouldn't be carrying that much cash around on you."

Emily's eyes misted as she stuffed the money inside the small purse Logan had purchased for her. Strong arms came around her, crushing her in a bruising bear hug.

"Dammit, Em, I know I shouldn't let you do this, whatever it is."

She gave him a watery smile. "But you will, won't you?"

"Yeah." Cocking his head, Luke studied her. "You know, I always thought you needed some excitement to spice up your life." He frowned. "I have a feeling that whatever this is, it isn't what you need at all."

Standing on the tips of her toes, she brushed a light kiss against his cheek. "You're the best brother in the whole wide world, Luke."

"Yeah, and the biggest chump," she heard him mutter. "You take care of yourself, darlin'. And keep in touch."

"I will." Or rather Logan would take care of her, Emily silently amended. Of that, she was one hundred percent certain.

Once she was back outside Emily never paused, never once looked in the direction of the car she knew was parked down the street. Following Logan's instructions, she walked the two blocks down the street to the convenience store.

She hadn't questioned Logan's plan, the one he had made after making a thorough study of the area. Pausing inside the store, Emily searched for the rest room Logan said was there. Eyes forward, she walked to the back of the store, ignoring the fact that her knees were knocking together. Once inside, she locked the door as she had been instructed and leaned against it.

She had five torturous minutes to wait before she could leave and meet Logan in front of the store. She might as well make use of the facilities while she was here. Moving over to the single stall, she pushed open the

gray door, and got the shock of her life as Logan leaped
out. He clamped a hand over her mouth to prevent her
from screaming. "Did you get it?"

Emily nodded as Logan's hand slid from her mouth.
"Yes, I did. No problem," she returned excitedly.

He smiled sadly. "I really hate to burst your bubble,
but we do have a problem. A serious one. You were followed."

Chapter 7

"What? How? Who?"

He hated to be the one to wipe that look of exhilaration and accomplishment off of her face. He felt responsible. This morning when he had done his extensive recon of the area, he had spotted the two cars discreetly parked outside of Osborn's restaurant. He had seen the two sets of watchers. They had "Company Men" written all over them.

He had gone ahead and sent Emily in anyway. He had counted on the fact that those agents would not recognize her. Although Logan hadn't wanted to do it, there were no other options.

Now he had to decide if those men had actually made her, or if they had orders to follow anyone who had contact with Osborn on the off chance they might lead them right back to Emily and himself.

"Logan?" At the soft, worried tone, he realigned his attention to Emily. "How could you tell that I was followed?"

"Because I was following you. There were two men in a car opposite the place, and another two parked in a car on the side street. One set followed you from the restaurant."

Hurt skidded across her expressive face. Betrayal lodged in her eyes. It was almost more than he could stand.

Reaching up, he cupped her face, gently fanning his fingers across her cheeks. "It wasn't that I didn't trust you, Emily. I couldn't let you go there alone. I couldn't let anything happen to you."

Logan's breath came out in a low rush at her slow nod of understanding.

"That's why you told me to come here instead of going back to the car, isn't it?" she asked slowly. "Because you knew those men were out there."

"Yes."

"You took an awful chance coming in here. What if it hadn't been me who had come in just now."

A broad, smug smile spread over his beautiful mouth. It transformed his whole face from hard and intense, to devilishly attractive.

"I knew it was you the minute you walked in the door."

"How?"

"Oh, honey, I'd know those gorgeous legs of yours anywhere."

A shiver of excited pleasure slid down her back at the unexpected compliment. Even calling her by the rather generic name of honey, no longer bothered her. Not when it was said so softly, so sweetly.

Hot color flowed into her cheeks when she realized just where her thoughts were leading. Her head snapped up when she remembered the men outside were waiting to follow her.

"Oh, Logan, do you think those men recognized me?"

He hitched one shoulder against the flimsy wall of the stall as he shoved one hand into the pocket of his pants. "It could be. More likely, they have orders to follow anyone who has contact with your brother. A long shot in case they could lead them back to us."

"So what are we going to do?"

"Punt?"

"I beg your pardon?"

Logan lifted himself away from the wall. "Once we saw our pictures on the news, I knew it could be in the cards that they would have men watching your brother's restaurant. Once I saw those men this morning, I knew there was a chance they might follow you. Now all we have to do is figure out how to turn it to our advantage so we can get out of this town—without any unwanted company."

Emily bit the inside of her cheek, feeling depressed, miserable. This was all her fault. Had she been more aware, had paid more attention, she would have never brought those men here—endangering Logan in the process.

Then she wasn't very adept at this cloak-and-dagger business. Although she had managed to obtain funds for him, all in all, she was turning out to be more of a liability than an asset.

Emily turned the whole situation over in her mind and came up with what was the only logical solution. "I guess since I led those men to you," she began tentatively, "you'll want me to lead them away from you."

"No. In fact, I want you to lead them straight to me."

"Are you crazy?" Emily burst out in astonishment. "That's insane, dangerous. I thought the whole point of all this was to avoid those men."

That clever mouth of his tipped into a sly grin. "Sometimes the best way to hide is in plain sight."

She didn't understand. It sounded as if Logan wanted to play some kind of dangerous game with those men. A daring, bold game that had no logic, no rules.

"You *are* crazy," she breathed.

Logan's chuckle was soft, highly amused. "It's called misdirection, Emily. Magicians use it all the time. It keeps the audience's attention on one hand, while the other is performing the trick. In plain sight."

"I don't understand."

"Actually, it's quite simple really." His hands rose to lightly cup her shoulders. "You and I are going to create an illusion. We're going to convince those men of something other than the truth. To convince them that we are harmless, to allow us to make a clean escape."

"How?"

"By getting them to think that you are nothing more than a good-time girl who can be had for the right price."

She hadn't, of course, heard him right, Emily decided. If she had, then he was asking her to...

"I beg your pardon," she retorted stiffly.

That cynical, hateful smile was back on his face. Oh yes, she had heard him correctly, after all. He was actually asking her to...

"In a few short minutes, you're going to waltz that pretty little tail of yours over to the coffee shop next door and park it on a stool at the counter. A brash, gray-haired traveling salesman is going to enter later and capture your attention. You're going to flirt with him, cuddle up to him, and after a slow, sizzling meal, leave with him.''

The hands on her shoulders tightened. ''While those two bozos are waiting outside the motel playing voyeurs, believing we are set for a bit of afternoon fun and games, we're going to slip out of the bathroom window and be gone before they realize it.''

Speechless. Emily had just learned the true meaning of the word. She couldn't scrape two words together if her life depended upon it.

In essence, Logan was asking her to act like a prostitute. He wanted to throw those men off balance, off guard, off their track. He wanted her to flirt, to act coy, to be bold and sexy. None of which she had ever learned to be. He wanted her to...

''I can't do that.''

''Sure you can,'' he crooned. ''It's all very simple.''

She shook her head in denial. ''I mean I can try, but I won't be very convincing. I'm not... I can't....'' She sputtered to a halt and bit the inside of her cheek. She felt absolutely wretched. The one thing Logan had asked of her and she couldn't do it.

''I can't be... I'm not... very sexy,'' she confessed miserably.

Logan drew back his head, and thoughtfully studied her. ''Ah, Emily, of course you are. All you have to do is twitch those luscious hips and bat those baby-blues, and you'll have those men wishing it were them you'd chosen for a bit of afternoon delight.''

Those hands that had firmly grasped her shoulders gentled as they slid up and down her bare arms. Both thumbs sneaked out to glide over her collarbone, dripped down to the soft swell of her breasts left exposed by the low-cut bodice.

"Misdirection," Logan whispered in a low, gruff voice. "They'll see the hesitation, the innocence and believe it's the act, the disguise, the illusion. It won't even occur to them that it's not the reality."

Emily's fingers tightened on her purse. "You don't understand. I've never flirted with a man. I never learned how."

Logan straightened, his expression once again turning hard, impassive. "I think I understand all too well. I don't know where you got the idea that you aren't pretty, sexy, or passionate." One hand journeyed up the side of her neck, and his fingers curled around it. He used the rough pad of his thumb to lift her chin, making it impossible for her to avoid looking at him.

Those dark eyes probed deeply into hers. "Perhaps it was those puritan parents of yours," he murmured thoughtfully. "Or maybe it was that wimp of an ex-fiancé. But it's there. The heat, the fire, the passion. It may be suppressed by that timid, prim facade, but it's there."

Her eyes widened.

"You don't believe me?" he went on in a silky smooth voice. "Shall I prove it to you then?"

Logan crowded up against her, pushing her right to the stall wall. Emily's mouth went dry, and her fingers frantically dug into the soft sides of the purse.

There was nothing put-on about this kiss. It wasn't done merely for show, for a diversion. This time, Logan didn't bother to tease. He ravaged her mouth with those smooth, firm lips, that roughly wet tongue.

Emily moaned, her lips parting to allow him access. Logan didn't even hesitate, sweeping his tongue inside her mouth as if he had every right. Once inside, he explored casually, coaxing her tongue to mate with his as he probed at the soft tissue of her cheeks. In and out, it darted, quickly, forcefully. Pushing up against Emily, Logan imprinted that hard body against hers.

He didn't taunt or tease. Logan took. One hand came up to roughly cover her breast. He kneaded and pinched and molded, learning it's shape, it's flexibility, it's softness. And then he redefined it.

Slipping a strap off of her shoulder, he drew it down her arm, exposing the hot swelling flesh. His mouth dipped down to nip, to taunt, to suckle until Emily's insides turned into molten lava, her knees to jelly.

Her soft cry was captured by his mouth as he ruthlessly explored inside. One hand slid up under her dress to gently cup the moist feminine heat that had suddenly sprung up between her thighs.

Drowning. Emily was lost in a sea of liquid sensations. Flying. She was dancing on top of the flames. Soaring. She had broken free of earthly bonds and floated among the clouds. Emily's lashes fluttered open as Logan lifted his head.

"If you weren't passionate or sensual, then you wouldn't respond so sweetly, so swiftly to this." He moved his hand, and Emily felt a jagged bolt of lightning streak past the juncture of her thighs to burn deeply inside her womb. She stopped breathing.

"If there was no fire inside of you, then I wouldn't get so hot, so hard, that I could completely forget we're standing in a public rest room and take you against this wall."

Logan pushed his hips against her, rubbing, making hard tight circles. Emily felt his unmistakable arousal as it pressed against her belly. Her breath came out in a rush.

"If you weren't such a sweet, sexy thing, then there wouldn't be this fever inside me, I wouldn't burn for you so badly. I wouldn't ache to taste fully of your trusting innocence."

He fitted his mouth over hers and drank deeply. Once. Twice. Again he pressed his lips to hers.

"It's there inside you, Emily," he breathed against her lips. "It always has been."

As he suddenly moved away, Emily felt bereft of his warmth. "And there's so much more inside you," he went on in a deadly serious tone. "There's a strength that's tough as nails. And courage. To go ahead and do what has to be done."

Emily was totally stunned by his words. This man wanted her. She had never had a man burn for her or be so achingly honest in his need. Never had she so yearned, so wanted to quench a man's fire—or to surrender to the flame that was roaring inside her.

Certainly not with Jacob, the only man she had ever been with intimately. The only thing he had ever aroused in her was embarrassment, disgust. He had turned something that should have been a very special moment in her life into something furtive, fumbling, with about as much dignity as a quick coupling in the back seat of a car.

This man had made it seem special, made her seem special. He made her believe that she was the only woman in the world he wanted. Never had anyone told her she was strong, that she was a woman of courage. And never had she so badly wanted to believe that.

"I have faith in you, Emily," she heard that silken voice whisper in her ear. "You can do it," he repeated, pushing away from her. "Now go."

In a daze, Emily floated through the convenience store, oblivious to the admiring appraisal of the young clerk at the checkout counter. She didn't realize that her cheeks glowed with a becoming pink or that her lips were still moist and swollen from Logan's explosive mouth. She had no idea her hair was tousled, leading the young clerk to believe that the foxy chick gliding through his store must have come from some lucky man's bed—or was ready to tumble into one.

She only knew that the dark, compelling man she had just left wanted her. That he had thought her to be a desirable woman, one who made him ache.

As she drifted out the door, Emily thought she must be walking on clouds. It never occurred to her to look for the men who were supposed to be following her.

Feeling lighter than air, she drifted into the café next door and slid onto a stool at the counter. The smile she gave to the world-weary waitress, who casually tossed her a menu, was warm, but distracted. She was riding high on a wave of confidence, and never noticed the man with an ugly bruise on his forehead who slipped into the café right after her. Or the second man with thinning brown hair who joined him in a front booth a couple of minutes later.

In fact, she was so wrapped up in her bemused thoughts, she nearly missed the man who entered the café, a short while later. Not that there was anything really memorable about the dull brown hair that was dusted with gray. Emily might have ignored him altogether if the man hadn't drawn attention to himself with his cocky walk, his brash voice and his blatant comment to the waitress about a certain portion of her anatomy.

Her jaw nearly dropped as he sauntered over to the counter and plopped down on the stool beside her. There was no mistaking those black eyes as they raked over her body in a hungry appraisal.

Logan.

Emily immediately felt her face redden, recalling what had happened in the rest room of the convenience store—and her own wanton reaction. She tried to duck her head, only his silent warning reminded her of the part she was supposed to be playing.

Nervously, she licked at her lips, not realizing how the gesture lent credence to the illusion she was supposed to be fostering. Seeing the brief nod of approval and the look of reassurance, which was so at odds with the suggestive smirk marring his beautiful mouth, gave Emily's confidence the boost it sorely needed.

She leaned toward Logan. "New in town?" It sounded so trite, so phony to her ears. It had been the best she could come up with at the moment.

"Just passing through. You from here?"

She nodded, and gave him a stiff smile. For some reason her tongue seemed to be stuck to the roof of her mouth.

"Gets kinda lonely on the road." The idle comment was accompanied by a suggestive wiggle of his eyebrows, and Emily nearly giggled. "Sure would be nice to share a meal with a pretty woman."

She lowered her lashes. "Yes, I know what you mean. I do hate to eat alone."

"Shall we?" He grabbed their menus, then guided her over to a booth by the far wall. Logan calmly slid in beside her and threw an arm over the back of the booth. There was an instant heat generated by his fingers as he toyed with the thin strap of her sundress.

Logan lowered his head and whispered in her ear. "Put your hand on my leg and run it up my thigh." He held on tightly when Emily jerked in surprise. "They're here. In the front booth over by the counter. No, don't look," he ordered harshly when her head automatically began to turn. "Just cuddle."

She tried to make her body relax as she placed a tentative hand on his thigh. She was shocked by how hard, how hot a muscle could feel. Her fingers flexed instinctively when she felt him tense, felt the deceptive power in the lean leg.

"You're doing fine," Logan encouraged as he nuzzled her ear. "They're the same two bozos who broke into our room."

"How do you know?"

He could have given her a long, complicated answer about gut instincts. Or that he had excellent night vision and had recognized one of the men. Instead he gave her a simple answer. "One of them's got a dilly of a bruise on his forehead. It's a dead giveaway."

Under the cover of lowered lashes, Emily studied the two men in the booth across the café. They both looked so ordinary. Just a couple of businessmen taking time out from their busy day to enjoy a cup of coffee.

Emily felt Logan's hand tighten on her shoulder, and felt some of her tension drain away. She relaxed, her fingers lightly probing the powerful muscles of his thigh. So lost in her exciting exploration, she never even jumped when the overly endowed, bleached-blond waitress came to take their order.

"How about a couple of burgers and some coffee. That sound all right to you, Darla?"

Startled, Emily could only nod her head. Darla? Who in the world... The smile just slipped out. "That's fine with me, sugar." It came out sounding so natural, without thought.

It was as if she had stepped through the pages of one of those romantic adventure books she dearly loved to read. She fluttered her lashes, stroked, touched. It was as if her body belonged to one of those fictional heroines. She felt strong, alive and courageous.

By the time the meal was over, she really did feel like Darla. She never even blinked an eye at the intimate, possessive way he held her, or at the suggestive leer Logan gave her when he paid the check.

They strolled right past the two men in the booth and left the café, looking for all the world like two people who were totally lost in each other. Once Logan stopped on the street and pulled her into his arms to give her a sizzling kiss. She never even realized he used it as an excuse to expertly scan the area. Or that there was someone other than the two men, who was vitally interested in what the redhead and the man with the brown-gray hair were doing.

The minute they stepped into the motel room, Logan pulled her into his arms, turning Emily so that her back was to the window. She came to him so willingly, kissed him so passionatcly, hc nearly lost his head. Again.

Only a quick look out of the window where he spotted the dark sedan, forcibly reminded him of the dangerous game they were playing.

It was bad enough that he had nearly lost his head back in the café over those eager touches and the hot promise in those innocent eyes. He couldn't afford to do it now. Not when everything was on the line.

Deliberately, he slipped the straps off of her shoulders, his mouth trailing down under her ear, along the side of her neck. He needed to make this a good show, needed to convince the two men watching that they were just two harmless people—only interested in an afternoon of fun and games. And he had to keep a clear head while doing it.

Logan reached for the back zipper on the sundress. In that instant, he knew he couldn't do it. He couldn't make a spectacle out of Emily while those men were avidly watching through the window. He crushed her close, using the motion to swing her around until she was totally shielded by his body.

"Reach up and pull the curtains closed, Emily," he ordered gruffly.

Fumbling, Emily jerked on the pull. The drapes slid closed. She reached for Logan again, only to find he wasn't there.

"Congratulations. That was a masterful performance. Those men are sure to be convinced we are now writhing on the bed."

Emily was stunned by the easy indifference in his voice. Hot color flooded into her cheeks. How had she forgotten that this was merely a performance, a show for the two men watching them? A cold wave of reality washed over her. She had forgotten, so completely, that if Logan had pressed, had taken her onto that double bed, she would have gone willingly. She would have surrendered completely. Without a thought.

"Come on, Emily, fix your dress. We've got to get out of here."

She couldn't seem to make her hands move. How could Logan act like nothing had happened? How could he not be affected by what had happened? In a daze, she managed to pull up the strap on the dress, rearranging the bodice he had dislodged.

Maybe he hadn't been affected. Emily felt the flush of embarrassment all the way down to her toes. She had crawled all over him in a public place. Dear Lord, she would have crawled into bed with him. A man she had only known for three days, a man who had dragged her halfway across the state, had gotten her involved in a murder and made her a fugitive wanted by the police.

What really shocked and appalled her was the crushing disappointment she felt. More than anything, she realized that she wanted Logan to pull her into his arms, onto that bed. She was furious with herself for feeling that way.

"Come on, Emily, get your tail in gear. We've got to get out of here."

Pressing her lips together, she followed him into the bathroom. There was a part of her that was amazed at how Logan could get those broad shoulders through that small window. Logan, it seemed, could do anything. Even mesmerize her into believing that a vital, dynamic man like him could actually want an unexciting, dull creature like her.

But never again, Emily vowed. Never again would she be so gullible, so foolish as to believe in an empty dream.

"Crawl through," she heard the whispered command. Automatically, she obeyed, pushing one leg through the now-screenless window. Logan caught her on the other side and lifted her through the opening.

"Come on." She started to comply, then stopped and cocked her head when she thought she heard her name being called.

Logan reached over and grasped her arm, pulling her forward. Emily stumbled as he hauled her over the unpaved ground. Again her head swiveled when she thought she heard the sound of her name.

Impossible, she told herself. Just a trick of her imagination that she thought she had heard her brother's voice. Just wishful thinking that Luke would come, as he had done in the past, to help her out of one more impossible situation.

Logan led her through the twisted, complicated mountain streets until she was totally confused and completely lost. Twice, he pushed her into the door of a shop where they would browse for a few minutes, before he would haul her out again.

After what seemed like hours, Emily finally recognized where she was when she spotted the dark green foreign-made car, the last in a long line of vehicles that Logan had so creatively "borrowed." With little ceremony, he pushed her into the passenger side of the car, before rounding the hood and slipping into the driver's seat.

"Keep down," he admonished harshly. "Keep out of sight until I tell you differently."

Emily folded her body into the compact space under the dashboard.

The powerful engine roared to life, and Emily felt the car move. She rested her head against the edge of the seat, and closed her eyes. She couldn't believe how tired she was. And how thoroughly humiliated she felt. If anything, this whole morning had proven to her just how far she was out of her depth in this terrible situation.

How could she have thought that Logan had actually wanted her? The man had all but admitted that he could tell her anything, and have her believing it in a matter of minutes.

What had possessed her to respond to the man as if she had been brought up with no morals, no standards? How could she have made such a fool of herself in the rest room of the convenience store, then again at the café? Perhaps her behavior at the café was excusable. After all, hadn't she been playing a part, creating an illusion?

Yet once they had reached that motel, out of the sight of those men, what had been her excuse for forgetting why they were there, what they had to do and just how dangerous this whole thing really was?

A sharp turn made by Logan had her careening against the door, and jerked her right out of her dismal thoughts. Without thinking, Emily raised herself to take a peek.

"Get down!" she heard Logan roar. Before she could comply, she felt something slam into the rear of the car, heard a loud retort.

"Get down! Can't you hear that they're shooting at us."

"Shooting at us?" Emily echoed in disbelief. "Who's shooting at us?"

"The men that were in the second car outside of your brother's restaurant. They made us. I don't know how, but they're on to us."

As if to lend emphasis to his words, another shot slammed into the rear of the car, causing Emily to duck clear under the dash.

How had it happened? she thought blankly. Had she not been as convincing back at the café as she had thought? Had she messed that up, as well?

A whisper of a name floated through her mind. Had she really heard what she thought she had? Was it possible that...

"I think my brother must have followed us to the motel," she heard herself say in a small voice.

"How?"

Instantly, she knew Logan was not asking how her brother had followed them, only how she knew this.

"When we were slipping out of the bathroom window, I thought I heard Luke calling my name."

Logan swore. Viciously. "I must be slipping," she heard him mutter as yet another bullet hit the car, shattering the back window.

"Hang on tight, Emily," she heard Logan yell over the roar of the engine as the car suddenly pulled sharply to the right. "We're in for a rough ride."

Chapter 8

Rough wasn't exactly the word Emily would have used to describe the wild ride through the crowded streets of Flagstaff. Fast, frightening or paralyzing would have been far more accurate. What made it terrifying was the fact she was riding blind.

Since no more shots had been fired, it led her to believe Logan was going deeper into the heart of the mountain community instead of away from it. Long minutes ticked by before Emily realized she could no longer bear not knowing. Cautiously, she crawled up onto the seat.

"Would you get down!"

Ignoring Logan's growl, she used the back of the seat as a shield while she peered over the top of the headrest. She didn't know that the seat was woefully inadequate as protection against a large caliber bullet, or that Logan was dying inside to see her so foolishly expose herself.

As she had expected, he was moving through the heart of the mountain town. From previous trips up to see her brother, Emily knew exactly where they were. They were heading north up the highway that would eventually take them to the Grand Canyon. On her left, she caught glimpses of the quiet, quaint campus of Northern Arizona University. It passed by at an alarming rate.

Suddenly the car jerked as Logan maneuvered it to meld with the traffic on the business route of Highway 40. A part of her was in awe of the way he expertly weaved in and out of the traffic. Another part was horrified at the terrifying speed that made her heart lodge in her throat, and had her clutching the back of the seat in a white-knuckled grip.

Emily's breath caught as Logan deliberately cut two drivers off in his race to get to the turnoff for the interstate. She felt the engine straining to meet the awesome demands Logan was putting on it, felt the terrible draft created by the missing back window.

She heard the high squeal of brakes as he cut another motorist off in his race to make the off ramp. Slamming her eyes shut, Emily muttered a desperate prayer as Logan took the entrance to the ramp—on two wheels. The small car groaned, paused for a fraction of a second as the wheels grabbed for purchase on the hot asphalt.

Then they were off. Amazingly, they were alive and the car was still intact.

Opening her eyes, they widened as Logan raced along the overpass. Expertly, he weaved in and out of the signs warning of construction—sometimes traveling on the wrong side of the road. Logan deftly maneuvered the car, and Emily felt her admiration for him grow as he raced down the ramp that once again led to the business route.

After one more hair-raising turn, Logan pulled the car into the parking lot of a small shopping mall. Quickly, they darted around to the side, out of sight of the street.

"Come on," he hissed, grabbing both her purse and the small sack that held their belongings.

Scrambling out of the car, Emily had to run to catch up with him. It took Logan less than thirty seconds to decide which car he was going to "borrow." Another thirty seconds and he was inside, twisting the wires together under the dash.

"Get in!" he growled as he stripped off the ugly green shirt. Emily crawled into the midsize luxury car.

Reaching into the sack, Logan withdrew Luke's shirt and shook it out, making sure, she supposed, there were no glass fragments caught in the folds. Slipping it on, he left it unbuttoned. Grabbing a golf hat someone had left on the dash, he jammed it onto his head, before slipping into the driver's seat.

In less than two minutes, they were heading out of the parking lot, going at a far more sedate pace than when they had entered it.

"Get down. And this time stay down." He shot her a hard look. "Don't even breathe unless I tell you to."

Emily didn't question the orders. She scrunched down into the area under the dash designed for the passenger's legs. Even though there was more room in this car than the last, she was grateful she was thin as she folded her body into the confined space.

Logan drove as if he hadn't a care in the world. With one arm propped against the open window while his fingers tapped against the roof of the car, he casually draped one wrist over the wheel. He was even whistling some tuneless little ditty. He looked like a man who had nothing more on his mind than a casual afternoon of golf.

Emily stared at him. Who was Trace Logan? How was it he could create such ordinary characters practically out of thin air? She shook her head in admiration, deciding his mother had aptly named her baby boy. There was a trace of everything and everybody in him.

"There go our friends," he suddenly informed her.

"Where?"

"In the opposite direction. It may take them some time to find the car we abandoned, but after that it won't take them long to find out what kind of car we're in now," he added thoughtfully.

It wasn't long before Emily realized what was on his mind. He stopped off in the crowded parking lot of a grocery store—right next to a car that was the same make, model and color as the one he had stolen. With Emily playing lookout, it only took him a couple of minutes to exchange the license plates.

Then they were back on the road again, heading west. They were fifty miles from Flagstaff before Logan allowed her to move up onto the seat. They were halfway to Kingman, racing along a side road in a different car, before Emily allowed herself to relax.

It was indeed a race, she wearily decided as she dully watched the hot desert landscape slide pass the window. And they were running for their lives.

There was still almost thirty miles to go before they reached the Grand Canyon, and Emily could no longer bear Logan's condemning silence.

"I'm sorry, Logan."

"You should be. The next time I tell you to stay down, do it."

Wearily, she folded her arms over her chest. "I meant about Luke. I should have realized he might try to follow me."

He shot her an unreadable look. His fingers flexed on the wheel as he relaxed his shoulders. "It's my fault. I'm supposed to be the expert here. I know all about brothers and their need to protect."

Emily ran her palms over her arms as a sudden chill shook her in spite of the late-afternoon heat. "You don't think those men will go after Luke, do you?"

"They won't do anything to your brother. They can't afford to call attention to themselves. Most likely, any questioning will be handled by the police."

Hardly reassuring, Emily thought with a groan. Getting Luke involved with the police was something she hadn't wanted to do. Her parents would probably blame Luke for the trouble she was in.

It had been that way since they were children. Noah and Sarah Osborn never believed that she had the nerve or the backbone to get into trouble—not without Luke dragging her into it.

"My parents are going to be furious."

Logan slid a curious look at the woman huddled in the seat. Furious was an odd word. He could buy worried or frightened out of their wits for their daughter's safety. But furious?

"They'll feel better once this is over and you're safe."

"They'll be appalled," she countered flatly. A sad, painful smile curled her lips. "No Osborn would ever help a man who kidnapped them. An Osborn daughter should never share a motel room with a man she's not married to. They won't ever understand how I could stand passively by, actually was a lookout for you when you stole those cars."

"You weren't exactly a willing participant."

"It doesn't matter. They'll never understand. My parents tend to see the world in black and white, in stark terms of right and wrong. They have a very precise code of behavior, and excuses aren't allowed."

A harsh, bitter laugh escaped as she continued. "In this case, I'm not sure even Luke will understand. He must have been shocked when he saw us check into that motel. After the fiasco with Jacob, I'm surprised he didn't try to break down the door."

"Who?"

"Jacob Ridley. The man my parents wanted me to marry."

Logan's lips thinned, as a shaft of rage shot through his gut.

"What did Ridley do to you, Emily. Did he make a pass? Become too insistent?" His voice grew hard, as cold as an iceberg. "Did he hurt you?"

Her eyes widened in horror as her body grew stiff. "He...he..." She passed a trembling hand over her face. "It doesn't matter."

"Tell me, Emily," he demanded.

She slumped against the seat, head bowed, shoulders sagging. "Things got out of hand one night. I really didn't want to...I thought it would be all right since we were going to be married..."

Logan snarled a crude word.

Emily's head jerked up in horror at what she had just revealed. "It was my fault, Logan. I should have stopped him."

"He forced you."

Logan sounded so cold, so unforgiving. Rather like Jacob when it had been over. Emily sunk farther into the seat feeling small, miserable and unclean.

"Jacob said it would have never happened if I hadn't put temptation in his way."

"That bastard. It was probably your first time, wasn't it?"

"First and only," she confessed miserably.

Logan wished he could have just five minutes alone with Ridley. Not only had the man turned something that should have been beautiful and poignant into something distasteful and dirty, he had shifted the blame to Emily.

One look at her hunched figure and he swore again. "He was a liar and a coward. Not only did he bulldoze you into having sex, the hypocrite probably felt guilty for having stolen your innocence. Instead of accepting his responsibility like a man, the weasel tried to make himself feel better by placing the blame on you. Temptation or not, he was just as responsible, maybe even more so than you."

Her head violently shook. He could see she wasn't in any frame of mind to accept what he was saying. She would, Logan vowed. Someday.

The best comment Emily could make about this dreary, out-of-the-way motel in the small town of Moab, was that it was clean. In the dim light cast by the single bulb, Emily stepped behind the water-stained shower curtain. As the tepid water slid over her weary body, she found herself grateful for the small convenience that other people took for granted.

As she ran the soap over her body, Emily wished she could wash away the exhaustion, the guilt—right along with the dirt. Last night Logan had broken into an un-occupied cabin at another out-of-the-way motel. The bed had been small, and the mattress had a dip in the middle of it. She had lain awake most of the night, afraid to move for fear she would roll into Logan.

She had discovered last night that there was something worse than being forced to share a bed with a stranger—sharing a bed with a man she wanted and couldn't touch.

Maybe, Emily reflected as she stepped out of the shower, Jacob had been right about her. Last night, she had wanted to tempt Logan, had wanted him to make love to her. Only she didn't know how to go about doing that.

Sitting down on the edge of the tub, she ran Logan's disposable razor over her legs. Luke may have told her about the birds and the bees, yet he hadn't told her how to be desirable to a man, how to get him to want her.

A feeling of remorse stabbed at Emily at the thought of her brother. Although Logan had assured her it was unlikely the men who were after them would go after Luke, it wasn't any consolation. Emily felt miserable for having gotten her brother involved in this awful situation, knew it would put a strain on the already-shaky relationship that her brother had with their parents.

Wrapping the thin, threadbare towel around her, she was once again grateful to be so flat-chested. Otherwise, she would be forced to put on her soiled clothes. The lavender dress that had made her look almost attractive, was now wrinkled, limp and sweat-stained.

Dragging the small comb through her hair, Emily sighed. She should have known Luke would never let her walk out of his office without an explanation. He must have decided to follow her, to see if he could get a clue as to what was going on.

Her face flamed when she realized that he might have witnessed their little charade in the café. Luke must have been enraged when he had watched them check into that motel room. He had been mad enough when she had miserably confessed her small indiscretion with Jacob. She'd had to beg, to physically place herself in front of Jacob to keep Luke from trying to rearrange the man's horselike features.

Emily peered at her reflection through the fog-drenched mirror. She couldn't quite believe that she had actually told Logan about what had happened with Jacob. It had been hard enough to tell Luke, and he understood about her parents, had been raised in the same atmosphere, with the same rules, regulations and strict moral code.

A frown marred her forehead as she recalled her brother making some noises about it not being her fault.

She shook her head. Jacob had said . . . Her fingers clenched around the basin. Jacob had said a lot of things after that one dreadful mistake. Was it possible that what Logan had told her was true? Had Jacob felt guilty? Had he known that he was partially responsible, and had merely panicked and blamed her? Was it possible that she had accepted the blame because she had felt guilty about sleeping with a man she hadn't really cared about?

It was, Emily decided as she turned away from her reflection, entirely possible. Guilt had always largely figured in with the way her parents had raised her.

Going out into the other room, she found it was as she had left it. Empty. Logan was out on some mysterious errand.

Whatever he was up to, Emily didn't think he would be back for a while. Casting a longing glance at the double bed, she wondered if she could lie down for a minute and gather enough energy to force her body back into her soiled clothes.

As she had gotten very little sleep last night, exhaustion won out. Securing the towel, Emily crawled between the worn sheets, intending to rest for only a few minutes. It didn't take her more than thirty seconds to fall into a deep sleep.

The trip back to the motel was long, involved and done cautiously, carefully. Although Logan was certain that no one would find them, he wasn't about to take chances.

Running a hand through his hair, he carefully probed the shadows of the parking lot and the area surrounding the motel. He had been certain that their clever little ploy back at the motel in Flagstaff would work.

How had he missed Emily's brother? His shoulders slumped. He was getting old. His laughter held no humor. Thirty-three years old, in the prime of his life, and he was slipping. A year ago, even a few months ago, he would have spotted the man.

His hand bunched into a fist. He had to find Jamie. He had a glimmer of an idea where his former partner might be—if Jamie was alive, and not directing the men who were hunting them.

As he strolled around the parking lot, he thought about the men who were after them. There was no doubt in his mind that they were mainstream intelligence agents. Which made it a solid bet that Lewis Pennington, the somewhat prissy, overly immaculate liaison for Control, was involved. What he didn't know was whether Pennington, like the Scaffers, was being used, was involved with the traitor, or was the actual leak.

Stepping inside the motel room, he immediately spotted Emily on the bed. Every muscle in his body tightened and grew hard when he saw that all she was wearing was a towel. Damp red-gold hair lay on the dingy pillow. The soft swell of one breast was partially revealed.

Inhaling deeply, he prayed she wouldn't move, hoped she would. He was thoroughly disgusted with himself for wanting his wish more than his prayer.

This was worse than last night when she had been fully clothed. They had lain on that small motel bed, both stiff as boards, both afraid to move for fear they would bump into each other. He had wanted to growl at her to relax, to assure her that he wouldn't take advantage of the situation. Only he wasn't sure that he could keep that promise.

Finally, she had fallen asleep only to shift and roll—straight into his arms. It was close to dawn before he'd gotten his hard body to cool down—enough to get some sleep himself.

Abruptly, Logan turned his back, trying to get some measure of control over his lustful thoughts and his aching body. It was risky for him to indulge in wishful thinking—so dangerous to have his concentration divided.

Who in the hell did he think he was kidding? Both hands dived into his hair as he rubbed his scalp. If she were ninety-nine out of a hundred women, he knew he could go ahead and indulge in the passionate electricity that sizzled between them. He could alleviate his sexual tension, and it wouldn't cause a ripple in his concentration—or his conscience.

The women he had known for the past ten years had been like him. They had known how to play the game, had wanted the same thing—a pleasurable interlude that carried no strings.

Not so with Emily Osborn. What little honor, what little conscience he had managed to retain over the last ten years, was telling him to stay away from her. He couldn't have her sweetness, her generous nature, couldn't use her innocence to drive away all the remorse, to chase away all the dark shadows that haunted his soul. He wasn't like her sorry excuse for a fiancé. He couldn't use her, make her feel ashamed and humiliated afterward.

He had already done enough to this woman. What had drawn him to her was also keeping them apart. Emily was so untouched by the ugliness, so unaware of the vile shadows that slithered around in the world. She was so unawakened, so oblivious to her own passionate fires. She was so unsure of herself, of the deep core of honest strength that lurked inside of her.

He wanted to be the man to ignite those passions, to slowly fan the flames until they were both consumed by them. He wanted to teach her the delights of the body, the depths of sensation and the heights of desire. He wanted to drown in her sweetness, to have her cleansing flame burn all of the darkness out of his soul.

And he wanted so much more. He wanted to watch Emily grow into an awareness of herself as a desirable woman. He wanted to be there to kiss away the tears of her disappointments, to share the joys of her triumphs. He needed to protect her. He wanted the right to love her.

Logan bent and gripped the rounded edge of the dresser. None of the tricks for controlling his body were working. Perhaps the story that had been spread to cover his return, had more than a grain of truth to it. He did feel used up, burnt out. He had given everything to this business, his name, his past, his soul. And had gotten absolutely nothing in return except a bitter frame of mind and a bucketful of regrets.

Slowly, he stripped down to his shorts. As he crawled into the small bed beside Emily, he thought it would be okay. Hopefully, he was far too tired to start anything. After a few hours of rest, he would be completely and firmly in control.

For a while he managed to resist temptation, until a small, sleepy moan shattered what was left of his control. Logan carefully gathered her into his arms. "I will keep you safe. I won't hurt you." He didn't know who he was making the promise to—Emily, or himself.

Emily drifted out of sleep slowly. There seemed to be a hot lick of heat in the pit of her stomach, a restless feeling between her thighs. She became aware of a heavy weight on her breast, covering her heart. A hand, she sluggishly realized as it absently stroked and kneaded her flesh.

Logan. Emily's eyes popped open. Warm moist breath skipped across her shoulder, cooling her flesh, warming her senses. One hairy leg was thrown over her thighs, and she could feel a hard ridge of hot flesh pressed against her hip.

Slowly she turned her head, and came nose to nose with Logan. He was asleep.

Carefully, she tried to ease out from under him. With a grunt of protest he moved, rolling over onto his back while dragging a large portion of the covers with him.

Emily glared down at her body in astonishment. She wasn't wearing a stitch of clothing. What was supposed to have been a few minutes' rest seemed to have turned into a deep, healing sleep. She felt better—not normal, just better.

Pulling the slightly damp towel out from under her, Emily used it to cover herself. A quick glance over to Logan, and her gaze got tangled up with the acres of chest left bare by the twisted sheets.

He really was a magnificent man. Black coarse hair curled softly around the sculptured muscles of his upper chest, fanned down into a thin line that bisected the flat, ridged area of his belly.

With a start, Emily realized she had never really looked at a man. Except for the time she had watched him shave, she hadn't really looked at Logan. She was scandalized by how much she enjoyed looking, wondered if she would enjoy touching as much.

Biting the inside of her cheek, Emily let her eyes wander. Dark stubble covered the lower half of his face, making him look rumpled, unkempt and a bit disreputable. A wisp of a smile softened the firm, smooth lips, making him seem younger, vulnerable.

With a start, Emily realized that Logan wasn't all that much older than herself. He had always seemed so mature, so experienced. Without that cynical smile, without the hooded gaze to age and harden his face, Logan looked so sweet, so endearing, so...touchable.

Just this once, Emily knew that she was going to indulge herself. She ignored the little voice inside of her that told her to get out of the bed and get dressed. Reaching out, she used the pad of one finger to lightly trace the broad forehead, to smooth out the tangles in the dark-as-night brows. Lightly she skipped her fingertip down the strong blade of his nose, stopped to linger over the high ridge of his cheekbone.

His skin felt slightly coarse, slightly prickly. Carefully, she outlined the soft, firm, mouth, trailed her fingers over the squared bone of his jaw to probe at the cords in his neck. Caught in the grip of her fantasy, she let her fingers tangle in the coarse mat of hair and explore the bronze flesh hiding underneath.

His body felt as hard as it looked. Emily became so fascinated with how pliant his skin was, like rough velvet over polished marble.

Logan was a beautiful man. She drew one finger down the arrow of hair to skim lightly over the washboard ridges of his stomach. Nature may have been responsible for all of the elements that had gone into making this man, but Logan had done his part to maintain them.

Her fingers stopped cold when they reached the wide elastic waistband of his shorts. Emily was aghast at the way her fingers inched to explore the uncharted territory that lay under the well-washed fabric. Never could she remember having such a fierce need to touch a man. A real man, not one of those heroes that only existed in the pages of a book.

She had never felt a burning desire to see what lay beneath Jacob's clothes. Nor had she ever been allowed to. She hadn't wanted to run her hands over his body, had merely touched him chastely—a thing done out of duty not need.

She certainly never derived the pleasure she got from touching this man. Nor had she ever experienced such a burning desire to do more.

Temptation. After all the sermons her father had given on the subject, Emily realized she had just learned the true meaning of the word. It was the path to hell, Noah Osborn had always warned. It felt like heaven to

Emily. She slipped one finger under the waistband of the shorts. And froze.

Under the palm of her hand she could feel the sharp tension in the muscles of his stomach. Emily raised her eyes, and immediately got caught in a fierce ebony gaze.

"You're playing with fire, honey. You'd better watch out or we'll both get burned."

Caught. Emily wanted to sink through the bed. Not only had she invaded his personal space and his physical privacy, she had been caught redhanded doing it.

She swallowed. Hard. "I'm sorry."

"Me, too. Sorry you won't be able to finish what you started."

Emily squeezed her eyes shut, and wondered if it really was possible to die of embarrassment. The worst part was she couldn't seem to remove her hand. Her fingers flexed against the heated flesh.

"Don't! Right now I want you so badly my back teeth ache, and my body is about to explode."

Emily's eyes flew open. "You want me? You want to have sex with me?" There was a part of her that was totally shocked by her boldness. There was a bigger part that needed to know the answer.

"I've never wanted sex. I've needed it. Taken it when it was offered. But I've never come so perilously close to making love to a woman—whether she wanted to be loved or not."

Again she moved her hand, and was inordinately pleased when he sucked in his belly. "What if...the woman wanted it, as well?" Somehow the coy, inviting words coming out of her mouth didn't feel unnatural. Suddenly, Emily didn't feel quite so shy, so embarrassed, so worried about making a wrong move.

She felt like one of those fictional heroines. Women who challenged their men, teased them, taunted them and matched them strength for strength. She was, Emily realized, halfway to seducing this man. It gave her a strange sense of feminine power that she wanted to explore.

"When the woman is you, then I gather up what integrity and good sense I possess, and I walk away."

She tried hard to disguise the hurt, but that slash of bright pain in her eyes was nearly Logan's undoing.

"Why?"

Logan couldn't quite suppress the leap of joy he felt. Emily Osborn wanted him. So badly, she had ignored what must have been years of strict training and morally upright, uptight behavior and allowed herself to reach out and caress him while he slept. Despite what Ridley had done to her, she wanted Logan.

Logan knew he had to nip this whole thing in the bud. He hadn't been joking when he had told her she was playing with fire. Or that they would both be burned.

The easiest, most direct way to do that, was to be brutal. With any other woman, that's probably the way he would have handled it.

Not with Emily. She was riding on the wave of newborn awareness of herself as a woman, of the natural power she had over him. It was as fragile as fine crystal, as skittish as a fawn. One word wrong from him, and Logan had a feeling that her growing self-esteem, her confidence, would take a permanent hike.

So Logan lay there, wishing she would take that slender hand off of his skin, praying she wouldn't. "This has happened before, you know."

Her brow furrowed as confusion skipped through her eyes. "I'm sure there must have been a lot of women that—"

Soft, amused laughter cut through her words. "I'm talking about you and what you're feeling now. It's called hostage dependence."

Her hand stopped cold on his stomach, and Logan bit back a moan of protest. He gritted his teeth. "Right now you're dependent on me to get you out of this mess. You feel grateful. Perhaps feel the need to repay me." He paused. "It's not me you're really attracted to. You'd probably feel the same way about another man who had dragged you through the same thing."

Emily merely stared at him. She had heard about such a phenomenon. How a captive could be so terrorized, so fearful, that they could actually become enthralled with their captor.

On the surface, she supposed that this might be a classic case. Emily frowned. She couldn't imagine ever wanting to touch one of those men who had watched them in the café. She couldn't begin to imagine that she would ever try to seduce either the dog-faced man with the bruise on his forehead, or the other taller, rounder man with the balding head.

Actually, she mused, she couldn't imagine her wanting any other man—not the way she wanted Logan.

Besides, Emily reflected, she really wasn't a captive. Not any longer. Not since the night she had tried to help Logan in his struggle with those two when they had burst into their room.

So that really didn't apply any longer. Or did it? Perhaps she was just rationalizing again. Perhaps she was just looking for an excuse for her out-of-character behavior.

Emily looked down at the hand that still rested against his skin. It looked so fragile, so pale against the bronze flesh. It looked so right.

Emily smiled softly, and lifted her head. "You're wrong, Trace. Absolutely wrong."

Chapter 9

The flesh underneath her fingers quivered and swelled.

"Don't!" The low, raspy command was not firm. It sounded like a plea.

Emily smiled faintly. Perhaps she had been too hasty in thinking that Trace hadn't wanted her. That he had held her, kissed her, touched her, merely to convince her that she could play a part.

A miracle to think that Trace Logan desired her as a woman. Boldly, she pushed her fingers farther under the waistband.

"Stop, Emily!" It sounded like a cry wrenched from his soul, but it was unconvincing.

"Why?" She watched him clench his jaw, saw his hands grasp at the faded sheet. He stared sightlessly at the low ceiling.

"Because if you don't, I won't have any more control left."

Her smile turned triumphant. "Good."

One hand snapped up to grasp her by the wrist. "Why are you doing this, Emily?"

"Because I'm afraid."

He swore harshly, succinctly. "That's exactly why you shouldn't be doing this. You don't owe me—for anything."

Emily realized she wasn't afraid. Not of Trace. Not of what she wanted and needed, not any longer. It didn't matter that she hadn't known this man for very long. It no longer mattered that she still didn't know why he had been forced into taking her. She cared about Trace. He had to care about her. Otherwise, he would take what she was offering—and damn the consequences.

Something was urging her to grab for the brass ring; otherwise, it might never come around again.

It wasn't hard to say the words. "I'm afraid we'll leave this place, part company and never see each other again. I'm afraid that I'll never again feel the way I do now."

Lifting her hand, she didn't care when the towel slipped down, baring her body to the gaze of a man for the first time. Gently, she placed her hand along his cheek, liking the feel of the stubbled jaw against her skin.

"I need you, Trace."

He groaned. Three simple, ordinary words, and he was lost. There was a part of him that had known he was lost—from the moment he'd laid his hands on this woman.

He hadn't wanted to hurt her. He had despised himself for terrorizing her. He had taken great pains to reassure her he wasn't a criminal, a bad guy. He had trusted her, relied on her, worried about her and sought to keep her safe. He had wanted her for such a long time.

He should have realized long before this that Emily Osborn was the one woman he would never be able to say no to—or to deny. Anything.

Logan raised tortured eyes, and saw Emily in all of her glory. It was too much, far too much for any mortal man to withstand. Reaching up, Logan pulled her to his chest.

"Don't let me hurt you," he breathed rawly.

She brought her hands up to tenderly cup his face. "You won't. You're incapable of it."

There was such trust shining out of those beautiful eyes, it hurt. And something else that Logan was afraid to put a name to. Emily trusted him. Completely. Totally. Without thought or reservation. It was why he shouldn't make love to her. It was why, against his better judgment, he was going to do just that.

Reverently, he ran his hands down her shoulders to touch the soft, pale flesh he had so briefly sampled before. His breath came out in a hiss as he felt her swell to fit the palm of his hands.

His conscience nagged at him to give her one more opportunity to change her mind. "I'm scared, Emily."

She stilled. "Of what?"

"That you'll regret this. That you'll hate me. That you'll come to your senses and believe this is all a mistake."

A secret smile played about her lips, so at odds with the solemn gaze. "Never."

He had lost, Logan knew, to a woman with trusting eyes, and a certain sure tone in her voice. Kicking off the covers, he gently rolled her to her back and brought his body, his lips down on hers.

That lithe body pressed her against the mattress, threatened to crush her. Emily welcomed the weight.

Parting her legs to cradle him, she ran one foot over the back of a hair-covered thigh.

He trembled. Emily was in awe, felt humbled, yet triumphant. She had never made a man tremble before, had never made a man ache—for her. There was such a magnificent power in that knowledge, a terrible responsibility. One she would heartily accept.

Like in a dream, Trace led her through a dance that was as old as man, older than Time. Shedding her shyness as easily as she had shed the towel, Emily boldly followed as she shut out the fear, the uncertainty. Now that she was free to explore him, she wanted to touch him everywhere—all at once.

She ran her hands over the taut muscles in his back, curved her palms around the slim hips. Brushing her fingers over the hair-dusted flesh of his thigh, she smiled when Trace responded with a growl.

He didn't remain passive as she continued her shy exploration. He swept his hands over her body to ignite small fires. When his mouth closed over her breast, Emily gasped.

"Do you like that, honey?" Trace rumbled.

"Yes," she hissed when he treated the other breast to the same loving attention.

Through light, phantom touches and softly whispered words, Trace erased the memory of the awkward distasteful caresses of another man. He lifted her to a spiritual plane she never realized existed. He was a fantasy, a dream, a ghost that glided over her senses, fired them, until she felt lifted from her body, no longer anchored to this world.

His fingers danced down to caress her hip, to lightly stroke the sensitive flesh on her inner thigh. A white-hot bolt of lightning streaked through her when he found the very heart of her.

"What do you want, Emily? Tell me what you want."

Only one word came to mind. "More. I want more."

One clever finger slipped inside of her and Emily's back arched. Waves of pleasure crashed over her as she lifted her hips to match his gentle rhythm. Then, just as she thought she would die from the pleasure, he joined them together, making them one.

Trace was no dream, no apparition. He was very real, a very solid part of her and Emily cried out for the glory of it. Trace stilled.

"I hurt you," he muttered through clenched teeth.

Emily's head moved restlessly on the pillow as she grasped him by the hips and pulled him closer. "Never in my life have I felt anything so right, so wonderful."

Logan felt his heart swell as his body began to move. Never in his life had anything felt so right, so exquisite as being nestled so tightly inside of this woman's body. His confidence grew when Emily's hips moved in demand as they met his slow, shallow thrusts. Boldly, yet tenderly, he moved more deeply into Emily, and smiled when he felt her gasp with astonishment, with pleasure.

"Trace," he heard her raspy whisper. "Trace?"

"It's all right, honey," he soothed, stepping up the pace. "Just hold on to me and let yourself go, 'cause we're gonna fly."

Tiny hands grasped his shoulders, and he felt that delicate body arch underneath him. It was time, Logan knew, to let it all go.

"Oh my," she breathed over and over again as Trace pushed his hands beneath her hips and brought them together, as close as two people could possibly be.

With each bold thrust of his body, Emily felt herself racing to a place where sensations were like the colors of the rainbow, so infinitely varied, so heartbreakingly beautiful. Her world splintered, her body shattered, as all of the colors in the world washed over her.

Emily felt Trace stiffen, heard his rough call and wondered if he too had miraculously found that elusive heaven on earth.

He wanted her again. Logan pulled himself up to rest on one elbow as he spread his fingers over the soft flesh of her belly. A wicked smile stretched over his lips when he felt the muscles tighten and quiver.

Emily had been more passionate, more responsive than he had ever expected. The boldness, the wildness had taken him by surprise. Perhaps, he mused, she had done more than just sell those steamy bestsellers.

His whole body tightened at the image of Emily curled up on a couch, her eyes soft and dreamy, maybe even embarrassed by the intimacy of what she was reading. Sweet, shy, sexy Emily. All of her passionate nature would have been wasted on a bastard like Ridley, though it amazed him that some smart man hadn't seen through the prim facade to her natural sensuality.

"Why a bookstore, Emily?" he heard himself ask. "Why aren't you married and raising a passel of kids?"

"I almost was," she murmured wryly. "My parents had very definite ideas of who Luke and I could play with, how we should behave, what we could do. Since we weren't allowed to do a lot of things, I spent a lot of time in my room. Books were my window to the world. I've never really been anywhere, seen anything, but with books, I could go anywhere, see everything, be anyone I wanted.

Logan stiffened, his hand stilled. He had thought that by reading about her in the dossier, and being with her, that he had known everything he needed to know about Emily. He didn't know enough; he really didn't know a thing.

"You wanted to travel?"

Her head shifted on the pillow. She felt vulnerable, more exposed than when they had made love.

"I've never had a real vacation. In fact, that first night with you, was the first time I'd ever been in a motel."

"You mean with a man?"

"I mean ever. My father didn't believe he could take a vacation from doing the Lord's work. The only time we went anywhere was to go on religious retreats. We'd either stay with another minister and his family, or with a member of his church."

"So the old bag was right," he murmured. "You've never had a real vacation."

"No, not really. Which was why I decided to go to Hawaii."

"Why there? Arizona's closer to the Caribbean. Why not the Virgin Islands or Bermuda?"

Her eyes shifted away from his. "It sounded exotic, but safe. I wasn't sure if I could handle the thought of dealing with a passport, or try to cope with a different language, or a different monetary system."

If he had needed a reminder of just how different they were, how far apart in background, attitude and life experience, he was getting a dilly of a one now.

Emily Osborn was far different from anyone he had ever known. Guilt bore down on him. He should have never taken her on this insane journey. He should have never tainted her with his touch. He should have never loved her.

"And I went and ruined your vacation." Pulling himself off the bed, he jerked on his shorts. "I'm sorry, Emily. I don't know if I can ever make that up to you."

Logan fled into the bathroom, before he could turn around and do more than apologize to her.

Once again they had been driving around for hours, in a dark blue four-wheel drive Trace had "borrowed" the previous night. Emily's smile was wry as she looked down at the black T-shirt and matching denim jeans Trace had provided. They were a far cry from the lovely, very feminine lavender sundress. At least they were clean and fresh, if somewhat drab and depressing.

Shading her eyes, Emily watched the giant flaming ball of a sun dip down behind the shaggy, windswept bluffs. The low-lying clouds were awash with every shade of red, ranging from the lightest of pinks to near-violent violet.

It had been cloudy for most of the day, and she had little idea in which direction they had traveled. They could have been in Utah, Arizona or even Colorado. For all she knew, they might even have been in western New Mexico.

The only thing that had relieved the boredom of the tedious drive had been the scenery. There was such a terrible beauty in the semi-arid landscape. There were subtle shades of colors to be discovered in the unusual rock formations and desert plants.

There had been few people to be seen on the back roads Trace had used, even fewer signs of civilization. The haunting isolation unnerved Emily. It was a deserted, forgotten place—solitary, constricting and utterly lonely.

A coldness trickled down her spine. Sneaking a peak at Trace, she wondered if he too was affected by the bleak, almost alien landscape. He was dressed exactly like her, in a black shirt and jeans. A sweat-stained straw Stetson was jauntily perched on his head.

One thing was certain, he was far more impressive in the sober clothes. This morning he had washed all the dye out of his hair. With the midnight hair, the dark, bronzed skin, and the black eyes, Trace looked as lean, sleek and graceful as a panther. He looked, as the teen-agers had so cleverly coined, like a lean, mean, fighting machine.

As the light and color slowly bled from the horizon, Emily decided she was tired. Tired of driving, tired of the silence, tired of not knowing where they were going, or what they were going to do when they got there.

She was still reeling from the fact that they had made love this morning. Glorious, mind-scrambling love that went far beyond anything that she could have ever imagined, or ever dreamed. They hadn't spoken since their conversation afterward, nor during the long hours since they had left the motel.

Emily glanced over at the silent, brooding man. Perhaps she should have thought to ask him if he would come to regret making love, come to hate her. That idea tore at her.

Pushing aside the depressing thought, Emily decided it was time to break the silence. "Where are we going?"

"To find some answers."

How lovely, she thought dryly. A short, cryptic, confusing answer that told her absolutely nothing. "Where?"

"I need to locate a friend of mine. Hopefully Jamie will be able to help shed some light on this mess."

A cold shiver of apprehension rippled down her spine. She couldn't help but recall the last friend of Trace's they had found. And the condition they had found him in.

"Jamie?"

"Yeah, Jamie." Trace's lips twitched. "I suppose you could say he's ultimately responsible for getting you into this thing." He gave her a long, measured look before returning his attention to the road. "Jamie's the owner of that apartment I took you to."

"But I thought . . . What about that man we found?"

"Kessler. Hank Kessler was his name. He was Jamie's partner." Trace paused and lifted a hand to the back of his neck. "Jamie used to be my partner."

"Then, is he your boss?"

"No. We work for different departments though sometimes we work together on things."

My, my, Emily thought in amazement. Answers. She had thought that she would never get any out of this enigmatic man. Here she was running into a basketload of them.

"What's your former partner doing out in the middle of nowhere?"

"I imagine he's doing the same thing we are. Running. Trying to stay alive."

"Does Jamie know why there are people trying to kill him? Kill you? Does he know who is behind this?"

"That's why I'm trying to find him."

"How in the world do you expect to find him?" she persisted, waving a hand at the dark, desolate landscape.

"There is a special place that Jamie goes to when he wants to get away from it all. It's also an excellent place to hide. I'm hoping that's where he's decided to go underground."

"So just how long is it going to take to get there?"

He lifted a shoulder. "Awhile. I've only been there a couple of times myself, so I have to rely on my memory."

Emily cast a worried look out of the window as the last gasp of daylight faded from the sky. "Are you sure you'll be able to find it?"

"Yeah, I'll find it. In my line of work, I've had to develop a memory with a great capacity for detail." He slanted her a reassuring grin. "Listen, why don't you try to get some rest?"

Logan watched as she folded her arms under her breasts and leaned her head against the back of the seat. With a console stuck between the seats, he couldn't offer his lap as a pillow as he had done before. That wouldn't be a good idea, not after what had happened this morning.

His grip tightened on the wheel as his mouth pulled into a grim, flat line. Waking up this morning to feel those soft hesitant hands on his body, to see the undisguised look of wonder, of hunger in her eyes, he hadn't had the strength to deny her.

Logan groaned and wiped a damp palm on his thigh. Not only had he had to fight his own wants, his desires, he had had to fight Emily's, as well.

She hadn't bought his explanation for the way she felt about him. Very calmly, very clearly, she had solemnly informed him that he was wrong. Then she had told him that she had wanted him. That had been the kicker that had broken the bonds he had placed on himself.

Making love to Emily had been more than he had bargained for. In Emily's arms, inside of her, he had felt clean and whole for the first time in a very long while.

He had felt at peace.

Logan raked a hand through his hair. None of this was going like it should. Logan dropped his hand to the back of his head. This whole thing hadn't gone as it should from the moment he had stepped off the army transport plane back in Phoenix.

He hadn't been particularly surprised that Garibaldi had met his plane, nor that he had been recalled to the States—not after that disaster in Panama.

The shock had come when his boss had told him why he had been recalled. Clearly, he could remember the bitter taste of betrayal when he had learned that his friends—the men he had worked with over the past few years—were slowly, systematically, being eliminated.

It all came back to Jamie. He had to find the man who had initiated the covert probe into Control. He had to find the man with the answers—alive, well, and not a part of the conspiracy.

An hour later, Logan switched off the engine. Despite it being pitch-black, cloudy and totally off the beaten path, he had found it. Or rather he had gotten as close as he dared to with the car.

Emily groggily lifted her head from the back of the seat. "Are we here?"

"We're here." He lifted a hand, placing it on her shoulder. "I want you to stay here while I find the man with the answers."

Emily blinked. "You want me to stay? But why?"

"I need to do some scouting. I almost walked into a trap before, I'm not about to do it again."

Emily felt a cold, ominous clutch of dread wind its way around her heart. "You think your friend may be part of a trap?"

"It's a possibility."

"But, but..." Emily paused, then she shook her head. "I don't think so."

Logan studied her thoughtfully. "Why?"

"Because of that man. The body. It's all tied up with this, isn't it?"

"Yes."

"Then if this was a trap, we wouldn't have found that poor man's body in your friend's apartment."

Logan shook his head in amazement. There it was again, that trust in things being what they seemed. In a way, Logan dearly wished he could count on it.

"What if you get lost?"

Logan flashed her a reassuring smile. "I'm an old hand at this. I won't get lost. I've found my way around worse places than this."

He brushed a knuckle across her cheek. "My brother and I grew up roaming around in the wilderness. Camping, tracking, survival, they were all a part of our childhood." His smile grew broad, almost sheepish. "Besides, my old man would kick my butt from here to China if I got lost and left a lady in distress to fend for herself."

Logan couldn't resist dropping a light kiss on those trembling lips. "I'll be back, Emily, you can make book on it."

Keeping the sound of the Colorado River to his right, Logan slid through the shadows. He used the natural barriers and the sound of the rushing water to cover his progress as he glided over the rocky terrain.

Fat black clouds billowed over the sickle-shaped moon, yet Logan had no trouble moving through the unfamiliar area. Instinctively, he knew where to place his feet so as not to make the slightest betraying noise.

There was an ominous rumbling in the distance. Logan used it to cover the sounds he made while moving through the sparse, prickly bushes. He had only been to Jamie's favorite place a couple of times. He felt confident. With his excellent memory for detail, a more than adequate sense of direction and experience in moving through the bush, Logan was able to quickly cover the distance.

Actually, he was more noted for his expertise in moving through concrete jungles, the war-torn rubble of Beirut, the jaded, sophistication of Paris, the hot, desperate slums of Managua. He was no stranger to barren deserts, the high country of the mountains, or the wild, raw beauty of the Northern Pacific coast.

There had been a time when he had looked forward to the annual trips he and Tyler had taken into the Canadian wilderness. They had been so young then, so cocksure.

It was odd, Logan mused as he ducked under a low-lying pine branch, that it had been Tyler, the brother everyone had considered the dreamer, who had made his adolescent dreams come true. While he . . .

Ruthlessly, he pushed the bittersweet memories to the back of his mind. Thinking of his family always brought on a severe case of the guilts.

Duty. Honor. Service. Those were the things ingrained in him since birth. It was why he had chosen the paths he had taken these past ten years.

On the nights when the dreams, when the remorse threatened to cast him into the deepest circle of hell, he would console himself by saying he had done what he'd had to do. What his parents had encouraged him to do.

How had he thought he could live without an identity, without ever having a place in the world? How had he believed that he could live the rest of his life as a nameless ghost?

Logan dodged behind a boulder as his eyes probed the darkness for any signs of movement. Even with all of his caution, he nearly stumbled into the camp. Jamie had gone to some trouble to camouflage his presence in the secluded glen. The sleeping bag had been stretched under a small tree, backed up to a small bluff. Not only would the overhanging branches give him some protection from the elements, anyone who would want to surprise him from above would have to go through twisted limbs and spiky needles to do it.

There was no sign of a tent, nor had Logan expected to see one. Jamie didn't care for the false security provided by an enclosed place. He liked to be able to see, and to hear whatever was coming—whether it be two-legged or four. It was a sentiment Logan echoed. He never stayed in a place that had less than adequate visibility, that didn't have at least one avenue of escape. He preferred more than one.

Quietly, Logan circled the camp, studying it from all angles. He had seen the oversized lump in the sleeping bag, had heard absolutely nothing. Yet he had a feeling about this. A very bad feeling. All of his finely honed instincts were clamoring, were screaming at him to leave.

Logan hesitated, just a fraction too long. He heard a small sound that raised the hair up on the back of his neck, and sent his pulse to hammering.

"Well, me boyo, you sure took your own sweet time getting here." Logan was able to breathe again at the phony lilting accent. With his bristling red hair and misty blue eyes, Jamie O'Connel might have looked as if he had just stepped right out of the Emerald Isle. In truth, his former partner had never set one foot in Ireland.

Relief coursed through his veins. His friend was here. The one man he had always thought he could trust, could depend on, was alive." Jamie?"

"Tis I." Logan took one step forward. "Don't move." All of Logan's internal antennae for sensing danger was put on alert by the cold, harsh command. He ignored a soft rustling sound that threatened to pull his attention away from the shadowy bulk in front of him.

Logan mentally called himself seven different kinds of a fool when he watched his friend raise his hand. All of the muscles in his body locked as he found himself staring right into the barrel of a gun.

It was hot, sticky and very confining in the car. Emily felt ready to scream. The far-off rumbling from the ominously dark sky set her nerve endings on edge, made her jaw rigid as she gritted her teeth.

Emily had absolutely no way to tell the time. She couldn't even be sure how long Trace had been gone. It could have been a few minutes. It could have been an hour. It felt like an eternity.

Despite Trace's assurances, she had spent the time imagining all of the things that could go wrong. She was a dreamer, a woman who spent her leisure time lost in between the pages of adventures, romances and mysteries. Somewhere along the way, she had acquired a very vivid, perhaps even lurid imagination.

What in the world was taking so long? In her mind's eye, she could almost see Trace as he moved through the inky darkness, see all of the hidden dangers that were just waiting to trap the unsuspecting: the unexpected drops in the terrain; the long sharp sticks that protruded from the ground; the thin, deadly snakes that slithered through the shadows.

What if Trace came across one of them? How on earth would she know? A shudder tore through her as her imagination kicked into overdrive.

Stop it, Emily admonished herself. Thinking the worst was not helping, would not make the waiting any easier to bear. She bit the inside of her cheek. What if Trace did not return?

Her worst fears were confirmed as another low rumbling sounded in the distance, followed by the sound of a gunshot. Emily scrambled out of the car, not giving a thought to how she was going to find Trace, how she could help him if she did.

Emily blindly raced in the direction from which she had thought the shot had come. A city girl by nature, by inclination and by experience, she didn't know that sound could travel quite a distance in the night, that it could become distorted, could bounce off the natural barriers of the landscape.

She merely ran, ignoring the small prickly bushes that reached out to grab at her clothes, to tear at the exposed skin. Her only thought was to find Trace.

As she blundered through the brush, Emily didn't take the time to think about wolves, or bears, or snakes—or anything else that could be slinking around in the night. She merely ran. Time had no meaning for her, nor did distance or direction. She was fully caught in the grip of a mindless fear for Trace.

The toe of her sneaker caught on an exposed root, and she went down, sprawling facefirst onto the rocky ground. Moaning, she used her palms to push herself up into a sitting position. Pressing a hand to her side, she slowly rose, willing the burning pain to subside.

Those fickle storm clouds in the black sky parted, flooding the area with pale blue-white light. Emily's breath caught in her throat, warring for space with her racing heart as two shadows detached themselves from the cloaking darkness.

Clearly, she could make out two men. One appeared huge as moonlight bounced off of the short, red hair. There was a shorter, dark man off to the left. Both of the men were training very nasty-looking guns at her still-heaving chest.

Trace. Even if they hadn't made love this morning, she would have known that shadowy form anywhere. With the speed of light, relief washed over her, making her feel weak and light-headed.

Trace was fine, and apparently wasn't in need of her help. Her eyes lowered as she took in the object that was directly pointed at her heart.

"I thought I told you to stay in the car, Emily," she heard him admonish. "Now you've gone and done it."

There were other words that Emily could not hear as a cloud moved once again to wipe out the last bit of weak light. It wasn't nearly as dark as the void that rushed to overtake her. Emily never felt the arms that caught her before she slid to the ground.

Chapter 10

The veil of darkness was slowly parted by a soothing voice, a caring touch. Emily became aware of the hard ground beneath her back. It was covered by something padded, slippery. The air around her felt heavy, filled with moisture, and she found it very difficult to draw an easy breath.

A burning image was imprinted on the back of her eyelids. That of a coldly fierce Trace pointing a deadly-looking gun at her chest.

A small whimper escaped. "Please don't hurt me."

Immediately she felt the withdrawal of that tender touch. In the rational part of her brain, or perhaps in the place where dreams were born, Emily wondered why she had said that. Trace wouldn't hurt her. Deep down, she knew that he would most likely give up his own life to protect her—or suffer all the miseries of hell if he could not.

Carefully, Emily opened her eyes to be greeted by that impassive stare. What had she done? Her thoughtlessly spoken words had hurt him. Emily wanted to snatch them back, and thrust them into the darkest part of hell—where they should have stayed in the first place.

It was far too late.

Emily tried to raise her hand, to establish some personal contact with Trace. Impatient with the weakness that invaded her body, she made a disgusted sound that came out more of a moan.

"Take it easy, me girl. Nobody's going to hurt you."

Her gaze shifted to take in the second man who was kneeling beside her. The soft light from a gas lantern turned the short, bristling hair the color of orange flame. The eyes were the most incredible shade of blue. No one would call the man handsome, not with that broad face, the flat nose or the freckles that liberally dotted the fair skin.

Jamie. Emily gazed deeply into the misty blue eyes and found a kindness there, a sense of compassion. It was at odds with her impression of the fierce warrior who had greeted her with a gun.

Suddenly, a broad grin slashed across the homely face, revealing a gap between the two front teeth. "You shouldn't have rushed up on us like that, girl. Near scared the boy and me out of our last few, good years."

Slowly her eyes shifted back to Trace. His expression hadn't changed, nor had he moved a muscle. "I heard a shot."

"That was me," the red-haired giant responded. "Keeping a nasty old snake from trying to taste the boy's leg."

A small, sad smile crept over her mouth. That musical, lilting accent was so at odds with his gruff physical appearance. A giant with a lyrical voice.

"Are you all right, Emily?" Trace's tight, rather toneless words cut through her fanciful thoughts. There was an intense pain in the knowledge that she had hurt him with her careless words.

She nodded. "I don't know why I fainted."

"It must be me face," the red-headed man bemoaned. "This ugly mug of mine has been known to frighten small children, make the little doggies dash away with their tails between their legs."

"You should have stayed in the car," Logan cut in sharply. "What in the name of all that's holy were you doing rushing in here as if all the devils from hell were after you?"

"I thought you needed my help."

"And just how were you planning to help me?"

"I don't know," she confessed miserably. "I just knew that I had to try."

"You've torn your clothes. You have scratches all over your arms, and got the scare of your life." His look softened, grew concerned. "You're bleeding," he whispered, reaching out a hand to a throbbing cut on her cheek.

He never made contact. Trace snatched his hand back as if he couldn't bear to touch her. As if she would burn him if he did. "You look exhausted, Emily. Why don't you try to get some rest while I talk to Jamie here."

Soundlessly, she rolled to her side and curled up into a small ball of misery. As the men moved away, taking the frail light with them, Emily knew she would have rather cut her heart out than hurt Trace.

The thought stole her breath away. How had she gone from being a terrified victim, caught up in circumstances far beyond her control, to a woman who had fallen in love with the very man who had abducted her?

That's exactly what she had done. She had fallen deeply, irreversibly in love with Trace Logan. A quick thing that had happened slowly, in bits and pieces. He had frightened her, abducted her, involved her in a murder, and with the police.

He had also comforted her, protected her and desired her. He had felt remorse and regret for dragging her into this situation, for spoiling her vacation. He had promised to get her out of it, to keep her safe.

And she had fallen in love with the man. Not because she felt some sort of weird dependence on him. Not because she felt gratitude that he hadn't hurt her in the process.

It was, she knew, because Trace Logan was a man worth loving.

Emily pushed all of those thoughts to the back of her mind. She was tired, physically, mentally, and emotionally. Only sleep seemed a million miles away. Overhearing Trace's next words jolted her wide awake.

"Would you mind telling me what in the sweet hell is going on here?" Logan stared at the man he called friend and waited.

Jamie sighed. "I'm afraid you know about as much as I do."

Leaning back against the rough surface of the bluff, Logan raised a leg, draping his wrist over one knee. "The only thing I know for certain is that Garibaldi recalled me from Panama because you thought you had found a leak in Control."

Jamie thrust a blunt hand through the red bristles of his hair, scrubbing at his scalp. "You remember the accident I had a few months back?" Logan nodded curtly. "Well, while I was recuperating, they stuck me on the board of review."

Logan chuckled softly at the look of disgust on his former partner's craggy face. He could well imagine how Jamie had felt being stuck behind a desk reviewing cases that had not produced the desired results. "You must have loved that."

"Near went out of me skull. It was why I was so primed when the report on Johnson's death passed over my desk."

Johnson, Logan knew, was the last agent to have died while on assignment. "You didn't think it was an accident?"

A crooked smile tipped his friend's full, broad mouth. "You and I both know just how precarious an agent's life is, how easy it is to die an ignoble, unlamented death. Accidents happen all the time, but it struck me as a wee bit strange that three agents had died in the last three years under circumstances that had nothing to do with their assignments."

Jamie lifted one massive shoulder in a careless shrug. "Johnson was a good lad. He once saved me life." The craggy face hardened. "He wasn't a careless man. It was hard for me to accept that he would get into a car that was mechanically faulty."

"So you decided to check further."

"I pulled both the files on Kelly and Randall, and found some interesting similarities."

"Such as?"

"That all three men were close to successfully completing their missions. That all three men were killed in seemingly innocent, unrelated accidents. That there were large quantities of coffee found in all of them.''

Logan studied his friend intently. So very little to go on. A gut hunch, he mused. As a man who lived by his instincts, Logan wasn't about to dismiss another man's hunches. "So from that, you decided that somebody in the department had burned those three men.''

"Kelly had an ulcer, Logan.''

His arm dropped from his knee as Logan leaned forward. "He had to give up coffee, didn't he?''

"The last I knew he had given it up in favor of milk, although he loathed the stuff.''

It could have been, Logan supposed, that the man had just gone off the wagon. With the stress, the constant fear of discovery that were part and parcel of the job, it wasn't hard to imagine that any man might say to hell with his health and indulge in something he knew might hurt him.

Any man but Kelly, Logan thought grimly. The short, slight agent had been a bit of a health nut. Kelly didn't smoke because he was afraid of getting cancer, didn't eat fried foods or much red meat for fear of having a heart attack. To drink large quantities of coffee, knowing he had an ulcer, was out of character for a hypochondriac like Kelly.

"So what did you do?''

Jamie lifted his hands, palms up. "The only thing I could. I went to Garibaldi. I only had a hunch, a bucketload of suspicions and no proper proof.''

"And Garibaldi's reaction?''

"He listened politely, asked a few pointed questions, and sent me on me way," came Jamie's dry reply.

Typical, Logan mused a bit bitterly. Ray Garibaldi was an emotionless machine of a man with a devious computer for a brain. Whether he had taken Jamie's concerns seriously, or had dismissed them out of hand, would have been a hard call to make. His boss rarely gave anything away.

"Two weeks later," Jamie went on slowly, "he called me back into his office. He had a wee story to tell me about a donnybrook that had taken place down in Panama."

Every muscle in Logan's body stiffened. "So he took your suspicions seriously after all."

Deep down inside, he had already known what had happened. Logan couldn't help the shudder of apprehension, of fear that skidded down his spine. The worst nightmare of any undercover agent was that his cover would be blown, leaving him open, defenseless, totally vulnerable.

There was nothing quite so horrifying, quite so capable of instilling fear into an agent's heart as the thought of someone deliberately betraying his cover— the very thing that made an agent so effective, that kept him alive.

To think that it might have been done by a superior, a man who should have been thoroughly trusted, sent a wave of anger and a sense of betrayal coursing through his veins.

"Do you know who it is, Jamie?"

"Possibilities only. There were only three men who knew you were down in Panama, who could have burned you."

"Pennington, Garibaldi and you," Logan deliberately supplied.

"The liaison between your department and mine, and the boss himself. Having Pennington show up at the

Scaffers' house the night of the meeting, swings the odds in his favor.''

Logan's head snapped around. "You were there? You saw Pennington?"

"Of course I was there. Have I ever missed a meeting with you yet, man?"

"I was watching for you, Jamie. I never spotted you."

"I was late to the meeting and when I spotted Pennington, I went around the back of the house for a closer look." A rueful smile stretched over his friend's mouth. "Like a rookie, I got spotted, so I figured I'd best be leaving."

Logan gave a quick nod of understanding. Jamie would not have walked into a trap, nor would he have wanted to lead those men to him.

"Do you really believe Pennington is the leak?"

Jamie lifted a shoulder. "Could be. He has reasons. He plays the ponies."

Logan lifted an eyebrow. "He's in debt?"

"Heavily. But I doubt he's the brains behind this."

"Why?"

"Because only one man knew about the meeting between yourself and me."

Garibaldi. Logan felt his blood run cold. He didn't realize he had said the name out loud until Jamie spoke. "Aye. Which would put him right at the top of the list. Except for one thing. He has very little to gain from it. Garibaldi has little use for money. God knows he has no life outside of Control. So what could induce a man to risk the one thing in his life that has meaning?"

No, Logan reflected, it didn't make any sense. Being the head of Control gave Garibaldi power. Power, he wouldn't jeopardize. His boss was far too smart to be lured by any promises of power in any opposition's operations. He knew, as well as anyone, that a man who was willing to betray his own people could never be trusted in a position of power again.

"Yet Garibaldi sent me to meet with you at the Scaffers', which turned out to be a trap."

"Makes me wonder if your boss might be a bit worried about the rumors that have been floating around lately."

"Rumors? What rumors?"

"That the powers in charge have been seriously considering retiring Garibaldi. That they've already got his replacement in mind?"

"Who?"

Jamie chuckled and rubbed a knuckle over a freckle on his right cheek. "You."

"You're crazy." The protest came out automatically.

Logan settled his back more firmly against the pitted cliff and thought back to that last conversation he'd had with his boss before he had left for this last assignment. Garibaldi had made some noises about it being Logan's last field assignment. He had specifically stated that it was time to bring Ghostrider in from the cold, and retire him.

Noises which Logan had ignored. Had his boss sent Ghostrider out on that last assignment as some sort of test? Or had Garibaldi sent him down there in an effort to quietly remove his competition?

"I see you finally figured it out. Garibaldi either wants us out of the way, or he's using you and me as bait. A wee bit of tempting bait dangled out to catch a very wily, very slippery snake."

Logan felt his stomach twist into a painful knot. "You don't know who is behind this, either."

"Not for certain, sure, although I'd be leaning toward Pennington. Garibaldi might have let slip the time and the place for our meeting, just to see who would show up."

It would be just like the man. Playing with two people's lives, tossing them into the lion's den without warning, just to see what would happen. This wouldn't be the first time his boss had used someone without their knowledge. Or their relatives, he added bitterly.

"It proves very little. We still aren't sure whether or not Pennington might be the leak, or whether he was being used."

"Exactly. Which is why we're still on the run. And on our own."

"Perfect. Just perfect," Logan breathed as he tilted his head back against the hard bluff. Briefly, he closed his eyes as a new thought struck him. "Does anyone else know about this place?"

"Only Kessler, and he, poor lad, won't be telling anyone how to find us."

"So you know about Kessler?"

He watched as the sadness washed over Jamie's face. "I heard it on the radio. I decided I'd best leave town. I'd hoped that you'd think about this place and come here."

"So you also know they're looking for me." Logan pinned his friend with an intense look. "Did Kessler know about your suspicions, your investigation?"

"That he did." Suddenly, without warning, Jamie's expression grew cold, hard. "I was to take the fall for Kessler's death."

Logan nodded slowly. Yes, it made sense, he decided. Why else would they have brought the body into Jamie's apartment if not to frame him? Only at the last minute they had changed their minds and had decided to set him up instead.

His mouth tightened. "Which one, Jamie?"

It wasn't his friend who answered. Logan went dead still at the soft, feminine voice that drifted through the night.

"Maybe Pennington and Garibaldi are in this together."

Even though the two men had been some distance away and speaking in whispers, Emily had strained to hear each and every word of what she had assumed was typical shoptalk, spy lingo. She got more than she had bargained for.

Nothing in her life, nothing she had ever seen, read or done, had prepared her for the story she had put together from the bits and pieces of the two men's conversation. It could have come straight from a spy novel, filled with death and danger, deceit and betrayal.

Only it hadn't just been a fascinating story. While average people ate, slept, had gone to work and lived their ordinary lives, men had been dying. They'd been betrayed by someone in power, a person who had sent them into danger, who they had mistakenly trusted to help them survive.

So caught up in the drama of the story, in the horror, Emily had forgotten that Trace had only talked freely because he thought she was asleep. She had been so eager to add her thoughts, she had inadvertently blurted one out.

Emily saw Trace's head jerk around, heard him curse softly, roughly.

"Well, well, little missy. I suppose you've been awake the entire time?" Jamie asked softly.

She nodded her head at the red-haired giant. Pulling herself into a seated position on the nylon sleeping bag, she tucked her legs under her and leaned on one palm, silently waiting.

"So you do understand that even if we catch the leak, it won't be the end of it?"

"Jamie!" Logan roared in warning.

Jamie tossed him a disgusted look before clamping his wide lips together in a frown.

"I don't want to put her into any more danger than she already is," Logan snapped.

Suddenly, Emily got the oddest feeling; she felt as if she had been dropped into the middle of a three-act play that had unexpectedly digressed from the script. What should have been a bit part for her at the beginning of the second act, had turned into a major role. She had little idea of what had gone on in the first act. Desperately, Emily wished she could sneak a peak at the last page, to assure herself that everything would turn out all right.

Only she couldn't. Because it hadn't been written yet.

She didn't intend to blindly blunder around until the final curtain—without ever knowing what had gone on before. Gathering up her determination, Emily raised her chin. "Don't I have a right to know?"

"She's got a point," Jamie observed thoughtfully. "To be sure, Pennington knows she's with you, and if he were ever to be getting her into his clutches, it won't really matter a whole lot about what she knows or doesn't know. Besides, since she's been awake the entire time, she already knows most of it."

Logan tore his eyes away from Emily's to run a weary hand through his hair. He was completely, thoroughly disgusted with himself. He knew he was letting his worries, his fear over Emily's safety cloud his judgment, and mess with his concentration.

It had been like that from the very first. He should have taken the chance that the Scaffer woman wouldn't have come poking around again. He should have left Emily right where he had found her—safe and secure in her own home.

Because of an error in judgment, things had changed. Whether he liked it or not, Emily was in this thing—right up to that pert, pretty nose of hers. He knew that with anyone else, he wouldn't have hesitated in keeping them informed, so they would not in their ignorance get them both killed.

So why not with Emily? Logan mentally cursed at the obvious answer. He had tried very hard to keep her from knowing what his job was really like, what kind of man he was. Because he cared too damn much. He didn't want to be the one to strip the illusions from those innocent eyes, to have them look at him in revulsion, in horror, to become appalled by the kind of man, that by necessity, he had become.

A thoroughly selfish motive, he realized—totally unfair to Emily. She hadn't asked for any of this. For the most part, she had handled every dangerous thing that had been tossed at her with courage and grace.

All she had really ever asked of him was that he tell her what was happening, and why. He had refused to answer because he had been afraid.

He knew that he had been a selfish man for the past ten years. He'd had to be in order to survive. This was the first time in his recollection that he had ever felt such remorse because of it. Or shame.

In the end, it hadn't really mattered. Because despite her need to believe in him, believe that he would not harm her, Emily was still terrified of him. The first words she had spoken when she had come around from her fainting spell had borne that out.

It hurt, Logan realized, with a deep-down-in-the-gut kind of pain.

"Are the Scaffers really a part of this mess? Are they spies, too?" Emily asked tentatively.

Logan smiled at the sound of disbelief in her voice. "Not in the strict sense of the word. Control uses their house occasionally for meetings."

Her eyes grew wide and round. "That's why you took me with you. You were afraid Dorothea Scaffer would come back to search through my house since she had been interrupted during her first attempt. She wasn't snooping through my things. She was looking for you."

"I told you I needed some time."

"But how did you know I'd be gone? How did you know my house would be empty?"

This was what he had been afraid of all along. That she would learn just enough to be able to put some of the pieces together.

Logan sighed. "As a matter of routine security, all of the Scaffers' neighbors were checked out. I knew you were supposed to be on vacation because it was in the dossier Garibaldi gave me."

Emily didn't know which stunned her the most—finding out that the refined Scaffers might be a part of a conspiracy to commit murder or that the government had a file on her. The color drained from her face. Just what kind of information had that file contained?

"What was in that file, Logan?"

"The bare bones. Just enough to assure the department that you were exactly who you claimed to be."

Well, Emily mused, she had wanted some answers. She just didn't like the ones she had gotten. Just how much did Logan know about her? Good Lord, had he known about Jacob before she had told him?

"I think that's despicable."

"But necessary," Jamie calmly countered. "The department doesn't send an agent into a situation unprepared. We always need to know exactly what we're up against."

A reasonable explanation, she supposed. It didn't help. She still felt violated. Knowing that there had been people poking into her personal life made her feel uncomfortable, angry.

"It still doesn't make it right," she replied tightly.

Logan had known all along that Emily would never understand that sometimes personal rights had to be sacrificed for the greater good. She didn't deserve to be dragged into the middle of a mess that she had no part in making. She certainly deserved someone far better than him. Which was why, once she was out of it and completely safe, Logan knew he would have to let her go.

Grimly, Logan banished those thoughts. "What in the sweet hell are we going to do, Jamie?"

"Unless you want to take a chance on Garibaldi, we keep on running. We keep on hiding. In short, we survive."

Survive, Logan thought in bitterness. Yeah, that certainly was the name of the game. It was more important than the job, more important than the mission. A dead agent was of no use to anyone.

Jamie's head tilted as he regarded Logan. "Maybe it's time we come up with a few surprises of our own."

"I'm real short on ideas, Jamie."

"What about your brother?"

Logan sliced his friend a sharp look. "Leave Tyler out of this."

Jamie ignored the warning in his voice. "He could—"

"No."

Leaning forward, with a grim look in the blue eyes, Jamie spoke, "It's not like he hasn't done this before."

"Forget it. That was different."

"Was it? Seems to me that it was just the same."

"Forget it, Jamie. Only you and Garibaldi know about Ty. I'd just as soon leave it that way. I never wanted my brother involved with my job, and I'm not about to drag him into this mess."

Jamie leaned back against the bluff, once again scrubbing a hand through his hair. "It's your call. I just hope it isn't a mistake."

"It won't be the first mistake I've made." His eyes flickered over to the brooding woman seated on the sleeping bag. He could only hope that it would be his last.

Emily fell asleep halfway through the ensuing discussion. Logan gazed at her reclining figure and pulled up a corner of the bag to cover her.

Poor Emily. Not only had she missed her vacation, she had been embroiled in a situation in which she was way over her head. In the past five days she had been forced to deal with things that would have been difficult for even an experienced agent to handle.

Innocent, trusting, sweet Emily. Logan gritted his teeth, snatching his hand away from the shoulder he lightly held. He wanted her so badly he could taste it.

He wanted so much more. Beneath that hesitant manner, the shyness, the lack of self-confidence was a woman of strength, of courage, of spirit. With the right man, she might be able to get in touch with the woman inside.

Selfish? Yeah, he had been selfish but not with Emily. She had touched something deep inside of him, something he had thought was lost to him forever.

Nobility. Honor. Duty. She made him feel like a white knight of bygone years, willing to sacrifice himself for the greater good. It made him want to duel with dragons.

It made him long to be able to dream again.

"What are you going to do about her?" his friend quietly asked.

Good question, Logan reflected. "Try to get her to someplace that's safe. Where Pennington can't get his hands on her."

Jamie's quiet bark of laughter was short, harsh. "To be sure, there's no such place. They're after her, every bit as much as they're after us."

"Then I'll just have to make sure they're too busy looking for me to go after her," he returned grimly. "I can't keep dragging her across the country. She's been a brick, through this whole mess. An exceptional woman. It's too bad she doesn't even realize it," he murmured.

"She would have to be, to have you fall so hard for her."

Yeah, Jamie was right, Logan knew. He had fallen for Emily. Hard. He had been tempted by her innocence, lured by her trust in things being what they seemed. He had been intrigued by her shyness, had come to respect her courage.

He had fought against it, only it had happened anyway. It had dropped on him like a ton of bricks—without asking permission first.

Even after spending five very intense, very compressed days with her under the most demanding circumstances, he still kept discovering new facets of Emily. He had a hunch it would take fifty years to uncover all the interesting corners to her mind, her soul.

Logan knew he didn't have fifty years. At most he had two days. It wasn't enough time. He uttered a rude word, frustrated over the hopelessness of the situation.

"So where are you going to take her?"

Logan smiled cynically. "To the one place nobody would think to look for her. My brother's cabin."

Jamie cocked his head, a slow smile stretching over his mouth. "A grand plan, since even Garibaldi doesn't know about that place. Let's hope it's enough."

Logan glanced once more at the sleeping woman. "It has to be, Jamie. It just has to be."

Chapter 11

Following Jamie's directions, Emily had no trouble finding the pool that had been carved out by the rushing water of the Colorado River. After spending the last two nights on the ground, she felt a desperate need for a thorough scrubbing.

Emily bit the inside of her cheek and gazed toward the rushing water of the river. Although this was the time of year people took advantage of the river's white-water rapids, Jamie had assured her that there were plenty of rocks and bushes to provide ample cover should any rafters float downriver.

Her gaze slipped down to the water of the placid pool. She had never bathed out in the open before. There was something almost scandalous about contemplating removing her clothes and sliding her weary body into the clear, smooth water.

There was no other choice, not if she wanted to bathe and wash her hair. Placing the bar of soap, the bottle of shampoo and the towel the red-headed giant had loaned her on a rock, Emily reached for the hem of the black T-shirt. Warm sunlight caressed her skin as she slowly removed the rest of her clothes.

Dipping a toe into the water, she was surprised how cold it felt. She nearly put her clothes back on. Gritting her teeth, she waded out to the middle of the pool where it was deep enough for a proper bath, yet still far enough away from the river's current to kept her from being swept away.

Forcing herself, she plunged her body into the chilly water. After that first gasp of shock, Emily decided that the silky water felt wonderful. It felt like sin. Goose bumps peppered her flesh, and her nipples tightened in protest at the icy temperature.

Dipping her head back to wet her hair, Emily reflected that it must be a sin to sit chest-deep in the middle of a river while the sun heated the exposed skin, and the water chilled the rest of her. It felt far too good. She would have liked to linger over her bath, but the prospect of having people float down the river, perhaps catching her as naked as the day she was born, forced her to rush.

Once out, she hastily dried herself, slipping into the T-shirt and a skimpy pair of panties. Winding the towel around her hair, she stretched out on a flat rock, letting the sun warm her bare legs.

She felt clean, refreshed and totally miserable. In a few short hours, before the dawning of a new day, they would leave this place that had become a haven in a nightmare world. By tomorrow night, they would have reached Trace's mysterious cabin. Then, after another few short hours, he would be leaving—without her.

Like a quail leading a predator away from his nest, Trace was going to leave her at the cabin, then resurface at a friend's house—drawing those men who were after them away from her.

That was the plan. Emily hated it.

She didn't want Trace to go. Not without her. She didn't want him to offer himself as a decoy, a sacrifice—to keep her safe. She hadn't asked to be in the middle of this mess. And she hadn't asked to be taken out of it.

In both cases, she had discovered that she had little say in the matter.

Emily had promised herself when the time came, that there would be no tears, no recriminations, no hysterics. Then why had she spent the last couple of hours wondering how she could seduce him into staying with her?

Frightened. Emily was scared right down to her soul for Trace. Hurting. She folded her arms around her waist, and bent over against the sudden onslaught of pain. Miserable. She knew she could not seduce him into staying. The only thing she could do was seduce him.

A rough blanket was suddenly dropped over her shoulders, and Emily jumped.

"You look cold. I thought you might need this."

Clutching the edges of the blanket over her chest, she gave Trace a grateful smile as he squatted down, placing one knee next to her thigh. Long, slim fingers toyed with a fragile weed, bending it before plucking it right out of the ground. In seconds, he had it shredded, strewing the remains over the rocky ground.

"Tomorrow night you can have a proper shower. The cabin's got indoor plumbing, and although the water pressure is dicey, at least it'll be warm."

Emily dragged her tongue over her lips. "Where exactly is this cabin?"

"A couple of hours north of San Francisco."

Searching deep inside herself, Emily plucked up the courage to be honest with this man. "I was hoping I could seduce you into staying with me."

Averting his head, he dipped those dark lashes over his eyes. "I can't, Emily. I've got to lead those men who are after us away from you. I can't risk your life anymore. When I know you're safe, Jamie and I'll go to Garibaldi and see if we can't find a way to put an end to all this."

That was another part of the plan that Emily didn't like. She had protested when he and Jamie had decided to take a chance on Trace's boss.

"I'm scared."

His expression softened. "You're going to be fine. Nobody knows that cabin even exists."

A hand rose, only to drop again to play with another slender weed. He wanted to touch her, to reassure her, but he wouldn't, Emily knew. Not with the thoughtless words she had spoken last night and her anger over the invasion of her privacy still between them.

Something inside of her broke loose, the fear, the impatience, the temper she hadn't known she possessed. She balled her hand into a fist and punched him in the shoulder.

"I'm not frightened for myself. I'm frightened for you, you nitwit."

Cocking his head, he studied her. "I've been in this business a long time. I can take care of myself, as long as I know that you're safe."

"I suppose you have. You're very good indeed. Maybe you are right in thinking that your boss isn't behind this, but you aren't infallible. Or invincible,'' she added quietly.

In spite of the efficient way he had handled things, Emily knew that he was just a man. He had wants, needs, desires. He had weaknesses, was vulnerable. He could get hurt, killed.

A shudder ripped right through Emily.

"I'll be fine.'' He brushed a light kiss across her cheek. "I'll get word to you at the cabin when it's safe. I'll try to explain things to your parents and your brother.'' If he was able to, Logan added to himself.

Emily frowned, shaking her head at this astonishing offer. How was it that a man could so frighten her, coax her into doing things she would normally be horrified to do, then turn around and worry about getting her into trouble with her family? Because deep down inside, she knew that he was a decent man.

"Luke will probably understand. He's been after me for years to put some excitement into my life.'' Her laughter came out sounding sad. "My parents, unfortunately, are a different story.''

She took a deep breath and forged ahead. It was important to Emily that he realize that in spite of his good intentions, trying to explain things to her parents was impossible. At the same time, she didn't want him to take the blame for something that was beyond his control.

"Because of their strong beliefs, my parents think that there are only two ways to handle things—the right way and the wrong way. Right from birth, they tried to set Luke and me on the right path in life, the *only* path, to their way of thinking.''

What was she trying to tell him? Logan wondered as he watched her eyes travel over to the free-flowing water. "I think I can understand that. My dad retired a colonel in the Marine Corps. He was big on discipline, honor, and doing your duty for your country." A smile curved his lips. "Although I'm not sure what I'm doing is quite what he had in mind."

Her head shook as her hand reached out to grasp his arm. "Luke and I were a disappointment to them. Luke always went his own way, no matter what my parents thought. And I . . ."

"Went your own way." One finger curled around her chin, pulling her around to face him. "Isn't that right?"

Her smile was soft, filled with denial. "Somewhat, I suppose. Although, if it hadn't been for Luke taking my side, I might have married Jacob and been miserable. I might have never opened my bookstore . . ." She ducked her head. "I've always been rather timid."

His eyes widened in surprise. He had known that her life must have been sheltered, perhaps even restrictive. He had never thought that it had been so rigid, so uncompromising.

Courage. Emily Osborn had more than a bucketful. It must have been so bewildering, so foreign to her nature, to have endured everything he had put her through, and not completely lost her mind.

Honor. The woman could probably teach his father a thing or two about the word. He had known that his kind of life was alien to her, almost incomprehensible, yet she had shelved all of her early teachings, had put aside the beliefs of a lifetime, and she had trusted him.

He, Logan decided, deserved to be tossed into the deepest part of hell for ever involving her in this mess in the first place.

Hearing the rumble of his husky chuckle, Emily raised her head.

"Timid? A timid woman doesn't constantly defy her captor, or try to knee him in the groin to escape. She certainly wouldn't have the nerve to order him to call the police after finding a dead body. A timid woman doesn't take out an armed man, then jump on his back instead of running for her life."

He dipped his head and shook it. "I've met a lot of people in my life, but I've never met anyone stronger, or so unaware of that strength. When are you going to see what's inside of you? When are you going to reach out for what you want?"

An excellent question, Emily reflected. A few days ago she would have said she wanted nothing more than to go on living her life the same way she had always lived it. She discovered that she had been lying to herself. She hadn't been content, she hadn't really been satisfied with her life. She had only been drifting along, taking what life dished out instead of going after what she really wanted.

It was the most outrageous, most inconceivable thing she had ever done, probably would ever do, but she wouldn't let him go on thinking that she was afraid of him.

Reaching out, she placed a hand along his bristly jaw. "I want to make love with you again."

Logan felt as if he had taken a blow to the gut. Over the years, there had been a lot of people who had needed him, had made demands on him, until he had dished out so many pieces of himself he feared he'd never be able to get them all back. Never had he ever wanted to give all of himself, whole and unsullied. Not like he wanted to give to Emily. How he wished he could be whole for her, wished he could give her everything she needed, be all that she desired.

Only he didn't have those things to give. Not even a few well-meaning promises. "Emily..."

A soft, sweet hand pressed over his lips, halting his words. "No, Trace."

His lashes drifted down, covering the confusing, shifting emotions he felt at the use of his name. How long had it been since anyone had called him Trace instead of Ghostrider, or any of the dozens of names he had used over the years?

Just a simple name, yet it conjured up recollections of his mother soothing his fevered brow. Or of the first time a girl had held him, had kissed him, had given herself to him. Innocence. It reminded him of a simpler, more open time. Hope. It made him long for things he no longer had the right to wish for.

Opening his eyes, he caught sight of the soft, secret smile playing around her mouth. His belly tightened in response, his flesh hardened.

"I need you, Trace, but there's so much more." A tiny pink tongue flicked out to moisten her lips. "I think you need me. You need to know that I believe you would never hurt me. That I trust you with my life."

It was more than Logan could stand. Rising, he lifted Emily and carried her to a sheltered place away from the river. After spreading out the blanket, he plucked the towel from her hair and combed his fingers through the short, flame-colored curls.

"Are you sure about this, Emily?"

She laid a hand on his jaw. "I've never been more certain about anything in my life."

He settled himself on the blanket and eased Emily over him, unaware that his smile was open, tender, and devoid of its usual cynicism.

"I'm all yours." Logan wished that could be true for all time. His smile broadened at the startled look in Emily's eyes. She looked as if now that she had him, she had little idea what to do with him.

She was, Logan soon discovered, a very quick learner. With a little encouragement, she began to explore him, slowly, hesitantly, but not reluctantly. He caught her hand and brought it down to his chest so she could learn about all of the dips, valleys and hills of his body.

Tentatively, she rubbed her palm over his chest, grew impatient with the dark shirt that was in her way. Awkwardly, she tugged it off him. Her expression was one of wonder and hunger as she gazed down at his bare skin.

"You are the most beautiful man." He writhed against the hard ground when she flicked a fingernail over one of his nipples. He groaned when she bent down to taste it. With his hands clenched into fists at his side, with his heated body aching, Logan secretly smiled as Emily reveled in the feminine power she wielded over him.

For a man who had learned by necessity to be selfish, it was the most selfless, most difficult thing he had ever done. His only thought was to allow her to have complete control over him, his emotions, his body.

For Emily, it was the most wondrous thing, the most precious gift anyone had ever given her. Here was a man who had learned, for the sake of survival, to rigorously hoard pieces of himself. Here he was offering all of himself—for her to do with what she wished. It was the most erotically exciting thing that she could have ever imagined.

Her fingers trembled as she fumbled with the zipper, and she felt immense satisfaction when she finally managed to open it. Slowly, she eased the tight jeans down over his legs, stopping along the way to pay her respects to the hair-dusted thighs.

Catlike, she stretched over him, slowly stripping off her T-shirt. She heard him groan as she wiggled her hips and removed the last remaining garment. She was rewarded for her efforts by the blaze of need that burned deeply in his eyes, in the stiffening of the hard body beneath hers.

Hot, harsh sunlight beat over their bodies. The fresh, nearly overpowering scent of pine mingled with the musty odor of the river. Birds twittered in the distance. The raucous cry of a hawk sounded as he swooped down to capture his prey.

Logan moaned when those slender hands curled around him. "Do you like that?" he heard her ask.

"You're killing me softly," he rasped in return, was grateful when she took pity on him. Rising, she settled down to take him inside of her.

Closing her eyes, Emily slowly rocked her hips, letting all of those incredible sensations burn right through her. She teased and taunted, bringing them closer to that burning ball of light that hung in the sky, to be renewed, reborn in the healing rays.

When Trace slipped his hand down to the place where they were joined to do some teasing of his own, it was Emily who felt close to dying. She felt frantic, edging ever closer to something that was just out of reach. Her smooth movement turned frenzied, greedy as she raced for the sun.

Then it was there, that searing blast that suddenly burst, filling her with pleasure. Emily reared back and uttered a harsh cry as she felt Trace grow taut and rigid.

She collapsed on his chest. Strong arms enfolded her as wave after wave of pure sensation coursed through her body, as her heart threatened to burst through the wall of her chest.

Minutes, hours, an eternity later, she tried to move, only to find that every muscle and bone in her body had turned to mush. Trace carried her back to the water. Tenderly, he lowered her into the pool and rinsed her off before returning to the bank to dry them off. It was Trace who bundled them into their clothes, then returned them to the secluded place that was hidden from the rafters who had come sliding down the river.

Sliding a palm over his smooth chest, Emily held on tightly as she settled her body next to his. In an amazingly short while, Trace's breathing evened out, grew deeper and measured. He had fallen asleep.

As the dappled shadows danced over them, Emily felt her heart swell, and she tried to swallow around the huge lump that had lodged in her throat. She pressed a soft kiss against his chest. "I love you, Trace Logan. Please take care of yourself. For me."

His arms tightened around her, and for one brief moment Emily thought that he had heard her quiet declaration. It wouldn't matter if Trace had heard her, she told herself as she drifted into a light doze. The only important thing was that he heed her plea.

Emily was rudely awakened when Trace jerked, dumping her out of his arms. A protest died on her lips when she saw a grim-faced Jamie towering over them.

"There'd be some activity on the road. We're in for a wee bit of company."

Jumping to his feet, Logan thrust a hand through his hair and uttered a curse. "How in the sweet hell did they find this place?"

"Must have been Kessler," Jamie answered tightly.

Logan lifted a hand to the back of his head. "I should have realized they might need more from the man."

Emily scrambled to her feet, dusting off her jeans. "Excuse me, but isn't Kessler the man we found in your apartment?"

"Aye. I think they originally snatched Kessler to see if he knew me whereabouts. Then, after they killed him, they decided to use his death to first frame me, then Logan."

The nightmare had suddenly, harshly, intruded on this place of peace. Her hand snapped out to snag Logan by the arm. "What about Luke? You said they would leave him to the police. What if they think he might know where I am?"

Looking down into her worried eyes, Logan could see how badly she needed to be reassured that her brother wouldn't share the same fate as the man they had found in Jamie's apartment. Common sense said that he couldn't give that to her. It seemed that every time he was around Emily, his common sense flew right out of the window.

"Luke's an outsider, Emily, not a part of Control. It would serve no purpose to kill him. Remember, he was alive and well when you left him."

It was such a meager bone, yet Emily latched onto it faster than a starving wolf. Luke just had to be all right. Anything else would be unthinkable.

"I suggest we make tracks out of here," she heard Jamie say as he tossed a dark blue backpack to Logan. He deftly caught it in one hand, and then slipped the straps over his shoulders.

Since going back to the car was no longer an option, they worked their way downriver—away from the road.

It was slow going. Emily's sneakers weren't suitable for rough-ground hiking, and the black cotton T-shirt and dark jeans were soon sticking to her like a second skin.

After a couple of gruelling hours, they came across a group of rafters who were taking a break along the riverbank. Emily was both appalled and awed by the web of lies Logan spun as he cadged a lift downriver.

She had lain with this man, had seen things in his eyes that he kept hidden from everyone else. Yet she hadn't believed him when he had told her that he could lie and have her believing him. He lied to those people and was so convincing, Emily would have believed him if she hadn't known the truth. It was a most disturbing revelation.

Riding in the raft was certainly easier than walking. And more terrifying. There were places where they glided along so smoothly, she could relax and take in the wild, breathtaking scenery. In other spots, the water was rough and uncontrollable as it splashed over huge boulders that threatened to tear the thin rubber raft apart—or any individual unfortunate enough to fall into the angry water.

Always in the back of her mind was the fact that there were men combing the wilderness, searching for them. Once when they shot through a narrow gorge with steep, impossible-to-climb sides, she spotted two men at the top, their eyes diligently trained on the raft. They seemed like ordinary hikers in their jeans and flannel shirts, but somehow they looked out of place.

Emily was terrified that those two would recognize them, perhaps even start shooting. She felt vulnerable in the small raft that could only go in one direction.

A hand fell on her shoulder, and she had to clamp down hard on her lips to keep from screaming. A quick glance over her shoulder, and she caught a glimpse of Trace, a small smile on his face.

Instantly, Emily felt better. Trace was right behind her, watching, keeping her safe. She held onto that knowledge all through the rough, somewhat dangerous ride down the river.

When the raft finally reached the take-out point, she was grateful to be able to feel solid ground under her feet. Once again Trace's silver and somewhat forked tongue got them a ride from the guide to the nearest town.

Sitting on top of the now-deflated raft in the back of a pickup, Emily leaned her head against the back window, out of the worst of the wind and dust.

A hand covered hers. "It'll be better once we get to town," Logan shouted over the wind. "We'll get some food, find a place to hole up."

"And a bathroom?" she asked hopefully.

"Logan grinned. "Yeah, and a bathroom."

Closing her eyes, Emily tried not to fight the bucking of the truck as it bumped over the unpaved road. It would be better in town. She was weak with exhaustion, with hunger, and she would kill for a chance to brush her teeth.

The guide dropped them off in front of a gas station in the center of town. Emily didn't have the chance to work the kinks out of her cramped body before Logan grabbed her by the arm, dragging her to the side of the building.

Plastered up against a tiled wall, Emily cast an anxious glance at Trace.

"You see them?" he barked at Jamie.

"Aye. They'll be up and down the road clear to Moab."

"Who?" Emily asked in a dusty dry whisper.

"Company men. Probably the police, as well," Logan curtly informed her.

It wasn't, she realized, any better in town. It was worse. Keeping away from the main street, Logan led them through a complicated series of side streets and back alleys while Jamie brought up the rear.

Finally, he stopped in front of an abandoned, boarded up gas station on the edge of town. She never even batted an eyelash when Logan pried off a board and broke a window. She had stood by before and watched him gain illegal entrance. Breaking and entering had already been added to her list of sins.

If it had been broiling out on the river, the bay of the garage was even worse. It was stifling, smelled of dust, rotting wood and old grease. There wasn't a stick of furniture in the place. Bracing her back against a wall, she slowly slid down to her seat. Knees bent, she rested her head on them.

"The water's off," Jamie succinctly informed them. He rummaged through a grease-stained box, withdrawing a rusty wrench. "This ought to do the trick."

Raising her head, she watched Jamie push his broad shoulders through the broken window. "Where's he going?"

Logan was at the door that led into the office of the garage, his eyes trained on the only window that hadn't been boarded over. "He's going to turn the water on. I did promise you a bathroom."

"He can do that?" A rather unnecessary question, Emily mused. Between those two, they could probably do anything they set their minds to.

It wasn't long before Emily found herself in the dark, airless ladies' room. She did her best to wash up in the stained, cracked basin. One look in the filmy mirror was enough for her to know she looked like something that could be found in the bottom of a refuse barrel.

Once back in the bay of the garage, she was startled to see Jamie dressed only in a pair of sweatpants. She hardly recognized Trace. He was wearing Jamie's clothes. They hung loosely on his lean frame, making him look gaunt and years older.

He came to her and placed his hands on her shoulders. "I've got to go out and get some things. Jamie'll stay here with you."

She knew that any protest she might make would be futile. "Please take care."

Dropping a light kiss on her mouth, he left her. Anxious eyes watched as he glided through the window. Emily wrapped her arms around her waist, willing the tight knot of apprehension in her stomach to ease.

"I wouldn't be fretting about the boy if I were you," came Jamie's soft reassurance. "Slipping through town unnoticed is mere child's play to Logan."

Not Logan, Emily silently corrected. Ghostrider. A man who could slip into a situation without creating a ripple, one who could slide out without leaving a trace. How could she have forgotten Trace's description of himself?

Gnawing on the inside of her cheek, Emily half turned toward the red-headed giant. "What exactly did you mean, Jamie, when you said that it wouldn't be over if you caught the leak?"

One wirebrush of an eyebrow rose. "That we have to find out who was buying the information. Otherwise, neither the boy's life nor mine will be worth much. Besides, what kind of patriots would we be, allowing a foreign agent to be roamin' around undetected?"

So it wasn't even close to being over, Emily realized dismally. Even if Trace and Jamie did manage to untangle this dangerous mess, there was still more to be done. And it was Trace's job to do it.

Her bleak gaze shifted over to the empty, broken window, as a black depression stole into her heart. How could she have missed what was so glaringly obvious? That there was no future in loving a ghost.

It took over two hours for Trace to return. Emily spent that time pacing the filthy floor, listening to Jamie's repeated reassurances that Trace could handle himself.

The minute his shoulders popped through the window, she wanted to run to him, to throw her arms around him and beg him never to leave her again. But Emily felt rooted to the floor.

Dinner consisted of convenience-store sandwiches, bottled sodas and small bags of chips. Although she had been starving, Emily could hardly swallow the dry sandwich, even though she washed it down with the lukewarm liquid.

They all spent a restless, uncomfortable night on the concrete floor, and Emily wasn't sure that she would ever be able to move when Trace woke her up at the crack of dawn.

In the ladies' room, she changed into the clothes Trace had gotten on his foray to town last evening. With a jaundiced eye, she surveyed herself in the mirror. The flower-print dress was two sizes too large and fell to midcalf. Huge pockets gaped in front, below her waist. Although she had never dressed in the latest fashions, preferring dark or muted colors and quiet styles, she would have never chosen such a dress. It made her look decades older.

Promising herself that she wouldn't ask where Trace had gotten such an ugly dress, once she was back in the bay of the garage and spotted him dressed in a pair of bib overalls, she knew she had to.

"Where on earth did you get these clothes?"

A cynical smile drifted across his lips. "Believe me, you don't want to know."

Which meant that he probably had stolen them. It was indicative of this whole escapade that Emily didn't feel the slightest guilt over this bit of petty thievery. What was astonishing was how fervently she wished that he had taken some other dress.

"Would you mind telling me why I'm dressed like my grandmother?"

Logan looked uncomfortable. Jamie, dressed in the sweatpants and a mud-brown shirt, shuffled his feet, looking like a schoolboy who was being chastised by his headmaster.

"Because in about an hour, we'll be heading for the bus station where a group of senior citizens are going to board a bus for a trip to Mesa Verde in Colorado."

Emily blinked. "You want me to stowaway with a tour group?"

"Yes."

"But what about you and Jamie?"

"We'll be heading the other way, in different directions. We're going to lead those men away from you."

Chapter 12

Catching sight of her faint reflection in the plate glass window, Emily frowned. Logan had streaked her vibrant red hair with gray. A pair of large glasses sat heavily on her nose, and her cheeks and lips were still chapped from yesterday's ride down the river. She felt as old as she looked.

Trace's hands closed over her shoulders. "You'll do fine. Just keep your head down, your voice low, and don't call attention to yourself."

Spotting his reflection next to hers, she smiled. With the dirty baseball cap, the bib overalls worn without a shirt, and the bright red bandanna trailing out of a back pocket, he looked like a good old boy right off the farm.

"Are you sure this is the only way?"

Turning her to face him, she saw the concern clouding his expression. "They've got this area boxed up tight, Emily. The only way you'll be able to get away will be if Jamie and I can lead them on a merry chase."

"But . . . I . . ."

He pressed a finger over her lips to halt her sputtering protest. "You can do this. I wish I could go with you, to make sure you get there safely. But I can't."

The pad of his finger drifted across her mouth as his hand curled around her jaw. "I keep telling you, you're strong, Emily. Strong enough to do what has to be done. When are you going to believe that?"

A slow smile touched her lips. She wished she could believe it. She didn't feel strong. She felt weak and frightened for Trace, terrified about what he was planning to do.

"Maybe if you keep telling me that, I'll believe it." Her eyes lowered to study the dull brass buttons attached to the straps on the overalls. "I never thought of myself as particularly strong or very courageous. I accepted long ago that I wasn't very interesting, just rather dull."

A raven brow rose as a slow, easy smile stretched over his beautiful mouth. "Not interesting, Emily? You've kept me guessing for days about what you were going to do. You've fought me, helped me and made love with me. That hot, no-holds-barred kind of love that most people only dream about. Oh honey, you're anything but boring."

Solemnly, she lifted her head, and Emily caught sight of the warmth dancing in the dark eyes. For once they were open, devoid of any shadows. Was it really possible that Trace was right?

Hands on her shoulders, he turned her around to face the plate glass window. His chin nudged in the direction of their reflections.

"Do you know what I see when I look at you, Emily?" he went on softly. "A lovely young woman who for some reason refuses to see that. I see a woman who can be counted on when the chips are down.''

Emily peered at her reflection, trying to see past the red-rimmed eyes and the dull hair that mocked her. Only eight days ago, she had been just an ordinary woman returning home from a grueling day at work. She had just been Emily Osborn, an embarrassingly thin, painfully shy woman whose sole source of excitement lay between the pages of a book.

A little over a week ago, she had returned to her home, had been caught and held, had been dragged over two states, had been embroiled in a murder and sought by the police. In eight short days, she had been terrified beyond belief, had willing participated in the theft of several cars, had been shot at, chased and had been on the run.

Cocking her head, she gazed intently at her reflection. Trace was right. She was no longer that woman. It wasn't, she mused, merely the different hair color. Her features certainly hadn't changed. Yet there was something in her eyes, something different, something older, wiser, less unsure.

One hand came up to lie across her cheek. Trace had done that for her. He had helped to turn her from a woman rather bewildered by life, rather short on self-assurance and self-confidence, into a woman who had dug deeply inside of herself. And she had found—much to her surprise—a woman of strength, perhaps one of courage.

He had given her a legacy, a gift that would be with her for the rest of her life. Never again would she be that woman who meekly accepted what life handed out to her. Even if she never laid eyes on Trace Logan again, he would go on being a major influence in her life.

Her smile was dry as she shifted her head. Emily was amused that a reassurance was trembling on the tip of her tongue. Usually it was Trace who had to do the reassuring.

Before she could voice it, a movement caught her eye. Over Trace's shoulder, she saw Jamie anxiously hovering in the doorway to the bay of the garage.

"We'd best be moving out now."

Trace's eyes never left Emily's. "Yeah, I guess so."

With a hand still on her shoulder, he helped Emily out of the window. Again he led them through the side streets as a fiery sun peeked over the horizon. It was a short walk to the bus station.

Pausing across the street by the side of a building, Trace reached into his pocket and pulled out a bus ticket. "Here. They'll be boarding soon."

Emily looked down at the ticket. "You knew about this last night?"

"I found out about the tour from a chatty convenience store clerk. Apparently his mother's going on it."

"And you decided to send me away," she returned, feeling some of her old insecurity creeping back.

Anger flared in his eyes and something deeper, darker. Regret. "I'll met you in Cortez, if I can. If not, I want you to get a flight into Denver. From there, you can get a connection to San Francisco."

Emily probed deeply into those dark eyes. Like a large boulder thrown into a calm lake, Trace had burst into her life, had created ever-widening ripples that would affect her for a very long time.

If it turned out that Trace couldn't make it to the airport, she knew that somehow she would survive. That was the legacy he had left her, that she could do whatever it took to survive.

Only she wouldn't allow herself to think that she would never see Trace again. After all these years, she had finally learned what both her parents had tried so hard to instill in her as a child. The belief that somewhere between human logic and skepticism lay something a person could never see, touch or taste. Faith.

Many a Sunday morning she had sat fidgeting on a hard, front-row pew, had listened to her father give a sermon on that leap of faith. A belief so strong, so enduring, that no amount of reasoning or scientific evidence could shake it.

That intangible belief had always seemed to elude her. Until now. It was there, hiding under the layers of knowledge and logic. It was why she had instinctively chosen to help Trace when those men had burst into their motel room. It was why, when she'd had the opportunity, she had not tried to escape. It was why she had so carelessly tossed that gun to him—without a thought.

Faith had allowed her to fall in love with this man, long before the bits and pieces of his life had fallen into place.

Reaching up, Emily laid a cold hand on his bristly cheek. "I'll be fine, Trace. You don't have to worry. You've already done enough for me."

She felt the muscles in his cheek bunch as his mouth tipped into that cynical, shadow-haunted smile. "I broke into your house, frightened the hell out of you, involved you in a deadly chase, ruined your vacation and placed you in dutch with your parents. Yeah, I'd say I'd done enough."

Emily's eyes twinkled with warm humor as she tipped her head back. "Well, it seems Fate has stepped in to put some excitement into my life." Her amusement slowly faded when a grim Trace carefully placed his hand over hers. "I don't think you realize just how much you have done for me."

There were so many things she wanted to say to this man. How grateful she was that he had turned out to be a man of honor instead of a criminal. That even though she had been terrified, that even knowing that she was still in danger, she would do it all again. Gladly.

She wanted to tell him how in eight short days she had fallen completely in love with a man who was about to slip out of her life nearly as quickly as he had smashed into it.

Trace shifted, and her glance fell on the white-and-red bus that would take her away from this place. There was so little time to say any of those things.

Pulling her hand away from his face, Trace pressed a scrap of paper into her palm. Puzzled, Emily stared down at it.

"What's this?"

"Directions to the cabin. Just a precaution in case I can't make it to the airport in San Francisco. I want you to go there." Gently, he cupped her face. "I don't care how you do it. Steal a car, take a bus. Just get there. It's the one place where I know you'll be safe."

Her fingers closed over the paper, crumpling it into a tight ball, as grief squeezed at her heart. It was almost as if he . . .

Emily shoved her fist into the loose pocket on the faded dress. She had to have faith that she would see Trace again. She would prove that the trust he had in her was not misplaced.

Hooking a finger under her chin, he lifted her head. Softly, he touched his mouth to hers. It was a gentle kiss, filled with promise, with hope. It was a kiss of goodbye. "I'll be at the airport, Emily, even if I have to claw my way out of hell to do it."

It was the longest walk she had ever taken. Emily kept her head low, her gait a shuffling walk, and resisted the urge to turn around for one last look.

She mumbled something to the driver when he took her ticket and carefully mounted the stairs to the bus. Choosing a place near the back, she huddled in the seat and stared out the window.

In short order the bus was loaded with the excited senior citizens and the other passengers. As the bus pulled out of its slot, Emily reached up and touched the window, as if somehow she could still maintain contact with Trace. Then knowing it was futile, she returned her hand to her lap.

A thousand things that she should have told him crowded into her mind. She wished she had told him to be careful. She should have thanked him for seeing her safely through this ordeal. She should have told him she loved him. Now perhaps, it would be too late.

About a mile out of town, the lumbering bus began to slow. Out of the window, Emily spotted a string of cars along each side of the road, saw something stretched across it.

Roadblock.

The hissing of the breaks sounded overly loud. One state trooper, his eyes hidden by a pair of aviator glasses, walked up and down on the pavement. Emily, head lowered, still kept her eyes trained on him.

"Ma'am?"

She jerked, and did what Trace had told her not to do. She raised her head.

"You'll have to get off the bus with the other passengers," the uniformed driver politely informed her.

"Why?" she stammered, noting that she and the driver were the only ones left on the bus.

"Just a routine check. Just be sure to have your identification ready."

An hysterical laugh bubbled up. Identification? That was the one thing she absolutely couldn't produce.

Knees shaking, Emily rose. Suddenly, she heard a roar, the sound of an engine being gunned. A long, sleek-looking motorcycle shot pass the bus.

"What the hell?" the driver muttered as he leaned over a seat to get a better look out of the tinted window. So did Emily.

She held her breath when the rider swerved to avoid the barrier. Clouds of dust billowed as he hit the shoulder and the back tire of the bike violently fishtailed. Positive the machine was going to flip, Emily fought against the scream that was clawing to get out. She released a breath when the tire found purchase in the soft dirt, and the bike roared around the parked cars.

Her grip on the seat tightened as she watched the bike as it disappeared down the road. Chaos ensued as four police cars with sirens blaring, tires screeching and lights flashing, raced in pursuit.

Trembling, Emily sank into the seat as the other passengers climbed back into the bus. She really should have known, should have trusted. She had seen the dark hair under the baseball cap, the blue blur of the bib overalls.

Trace had saved her once again. Feeling a desperate need to return to the comforting rituals of her childhood, Emily bowed her head, folded her hands together and closed her eyes. She prayed, harder and more sincerely than she had ever prayed in her life. Humbly, she asked for Trace's safety, for him to be kept out of harm's way. She prayed that she would see him soon.

Trace never made it to Cortez. Waiting as long as she dared, far longer than he had told her, Emily caught the last flight into Denver. She arrived so late at Stapleton Airport, the only available flight she could get for San Francisco was early the next morning.

She spent the night at the airport, tucked into an out-of-the-way corner. Pacing the small space of the boarding area, she could hardly wait to board the plane. The enticing smell of coffee from a restaurant down the concourse reminded Emily of her brother.

She stopped dead. How could she have forgotten about Luke? Recalling the expression on Trace's face when she had asked if her brother would be safe from those men, Emily felt a cold dread seeping into her.

I haven't really lied to you before, and I won't start lying to you now, Trace had promised. He hadn't lied, she believed, but had just neglected to mention that there was a possibility that Luke could fall into the same hands that had killed Jamie's partner.

She had to know. Glancing at a clock on the wall, Emily realized she only had a few minutes before the call came to board her flight. She raced to find a phone.

Searching the bottom of her purse, she came across some change. Her hands were shaking so badly, she could hardly fit the coins into the slot. Twice she had to redial.

"Hello. Hello! Emily? Please, if that's you, Em, answer me."

She never intended to speak with him. She had read enough spy novels to realize that there might be a trace placed on Luke's phone. Only the desperation, the plea in her brother's voice tore at her.

Love and concern won out. "Yes, it's me."

"Thank God," he whispered. "Where in the hell are you?"

"I can't tell you that. I only called to make sure you were okay."

"Me!" he shouted. "I'm not the one in trouble. The police were here, Em, wanting to know if I had any information about my baby sister. The one who was wanted for questioning concerning a murder."

"We didn't have anything to do with that, Luke. We only found the body."

"Found the body," he roared. "Dear God, what have you gotten yourself into?"

"I'll explain it all when I see you." Her head tilted as the announcement she had been listening for, finally came. "I've got to go now, Luke, they're calling my flight."

"No wait, Emily. Emily!" he shouted once more as she quietly hung up the phone.

Luke's frantic, furious voice stayed with Emily all through the uneventful flight. Even though she was anxious, she obediently remained in her seat until the plane came to a complete stop by the terminal. Consequently, she was one of the last passengers to leave. Even at this early hour, it was so crowded in the building, she paused, letting the traffic flow around her while she anxiously scanned the area.

How in the world would Trace find her? Clutching the plastic bag to her chest, Emily bit the inside of her cheek. He had told her what airline to use, but he had no idea which flight she had taken. Since she had waited so long in Cortez and then had been forced to wait for a flight in

Denver, it was possible that Trace had already been to the airport and left.

Emily found a small snack bar and purchased some coffee and a roll. Choosing a set that would give her a wide view of the boarding area, she forced herself to eat all of the sticky, overly sweet roll. Gazing down at the black liquid in the foam cup, Emily smiled ruefully. Waiting in airports seemed to have become a habit with her.

Time slowed down to a crawl. She tried to divert herself by indulging in some people watching. She kept finding herself searching for a tall, lean man with raven hair.

As it drew close to noon, Emily decided that Trace wasn't coming. Her hand slipped into her pocket to close around the piece of paper he had given her. He had told her to get to the cabin. He might even go there himself to make sure she had made it.

How was she going to do that? Stealing a car was out of the question. Even though she had watched Trace do it several times, she hadn't the faintest idea how to do it herself, nor did she think she had the nerve.

Money, she knew, was a problem. Getting a cab was out of the question, nor could she rent a car—not without a proper driver's license.

That left taking a bus. Emily went in search of a pay phone. Placing a call to the bus station, she discovered that a bus did indeed pass close enough to the cabin to allow her to walk the rest of the way.

As Emily exited the terminal and stepped into the bright, early-afternoon sunshine, she could only hope that her hunch was right. She could only pray that when she arrived at the cabin, Trace would be waiting there.

* * *

Emily's feet dragged as she trudged over the hard-packed dirt road. After spending a couple of hours on the bus, she had thought that she might enjoy the two-mile walk to the mountain cabin. She didn't, nor had she particularly liked bribing the bus driver into letting her off at an unscheduled stop.

Pausing on the soft shoulder of the road, she pulled the directions Trace had given her out of her pocket, and checked them once again. She had already passed the fork in the road and had taken the left branch. If she remained on this road, it should take her straight to the cabin.

Shoving the paper back into her pocket, Emily placed a hand on the small of her back and stretched. She was so tired. It was tempting to find a place to sit so she could rest for a while. Only the thought that Trace might be waiting for her at the cabin gave her the incentive to keep on going.

It was late afternoon before she caught sight of a building nestled between the tall pine trees. Her approach to the cozy, pinewood cabin was done cautiously. There was no vehicle parked by the building and all of the curtains on the front windows were drawn.

It looked closed up, forlorn and deserted. Emily paused on the graveled driveway. She had made it, but she felt no joy, only exhaustion.

Wearily, she mounted the three shorts steps that led to the door. The key was right where Trace said it would be—under a loose board on the porch. Quietly, she let herself inside the sparsely furnished living room. Bare, pine floors covered with braided rugs and comfortable, yet worn furniture greeted her.

Discovering the front bedroom, Emily dropped her things on a low chair and practically fell across the short bed. The adrenaline and the fear had long since deserted her, leaving her fresh out of energy.

She didn't bother to remove her shoes, or to wrap herself up in the old-fashioned quilt that covered the bed. She laid her head on the pillow and closed her eyes.

It wasn't quite dark when her eyes suddenly jerked open. She could very clearly hear the distant rumbling of an engine. Jumping off the bed, she raced to the window.

Emily only caught glimpses of the car through the thick needles of the trees lining the road. Her first thought was to run. Grabbing her purse and bag, she dashed through the bedroom door, intent on only one thing—escape.

She came to a skidding halt on a braided rug in the living room. What if it was Trace? Carefully, she made her way over to the door. Lifting the thin curtain over the small window, she peered out. Even with the lack of proper light, there was no doubt in her mind. The car was definitely headed for the cabin.

Long agonizing minutes passed as Emily gnawed on the inside of her cheek. She waited as the car came to a stop in front of the steps, nearly cried out when she spotted the familiar, raven-haired man as he finally emerged.

Joy flooded through her, along with relief. Both emotions were quickly overpowered by the sharp taste of fear when a movement in the trees lining the road caught her eye.

Her mind registered the crouching figure, the gun that was pointed straight at Trace.

Damp hands slipped over the knob as she desperately tried to open the door. She barked her shin against the frame as she scrambled out onto the small porch.

"Trace, watch out." The warning came too late.

He jerked around, leaving himself a clear target for the man in the woods. In horror, she watched the man aim the gun.

"Noooo." Her futile denial was lost as the shot reverberated through the woods. Trace was slammed back against the car, and Emily was in motion before he hit the ground.

Throwing herself to her knees beside him, her breath caught at the sight of the dark lashes that lay quietly over his ashen flesh. Blood oozed freely from his shoulder.

Four men came out of the woods, their guns pointed directly at them. Protectively, Emily crouched over Trace, determined to shield him with her own body.

A slender man with dark blond hair towered over her, a small smile tugging at his lips as he reached for Emily. Grasping her by the arm, he wrenched her away from Trace.

"Well, well," she heard him mutter. "Who would have thought that the great Ghostrider would have been brought down by a mere woman."

Emily's eyes slid back over to Trace. The breath was snatched from her when she saw that his eyes were now open and they were looking at her with dark suspicion.

Helplessly, Emily watched as the two men roughly deposited Trace on the couch inside the cabin.

"You got a first-aid kit?" one of the men asked Trace.

Those black eyes never wavered from the man who had brought her into the cabin. "In the bathroom cabinet."

The man skipped out of the room, only to return moments later carrying a small blue box with a red cross prominently displayed on the top.

"Let her do it," Trace commanded when the man reached for him. "She's bound to have a softer touch."

He looked toward the man still holding Emily, and the blond man nodded curtly. She knelt on the couch, her stomach turning over at the sight of all that blood. Her hands shook as she cut away a huge portion of the beige polo shirt.

She gasped when she spotted the large ragged hole in his back. "I can't handle this. He needs a doctor."

The man with the dark blond hair merely smiled. "We'll get him looked at once we're off the mountain."

Shooting Trace an apologetic look, she began to gently wipe away the blood from the neat hole in his shoulder. Her hand stilled when she heard him murmur, "Just do the best you can, angel."

Angel? Her gaze flew to his face, her eyes silently searching his. They were still as black as sin, still guarded and cloaked. Emily shook her head, astounded by what her vivid imagination had suddenly conjured up. It was ridiculous, insane even, but for one brief moment there...

"How did you find us, Pennington?" Trace asked the blond man.

"Why, through Ms. Osborn of course." Standing with his feet braced far apart, his arms folded over the front of the wrinkled suit, the liaison looked supremely confident that his prisoners could not escape. "She called her brother from the airport. Were were able to get her flight number and destination from the background noise."

"Clever," Trace murmured. "Why didn't you just pick her up at the airport?"

"The chief thought it would be best to let her go about her business. He was certain that she would eventually lead us right to you."

Emily's fingers tightened around the gauze she had been folding to make a thick pad. It had never occurred to her to check to see if she was being followed. She never watched to see if someone was overly interested in a woman in an ugly flowered dress.

"We spotted her at the airport when she got off the plane," Pennington went on. "Then it was a simple matter of following the bus she took."

Anger lashed through Emily. She had thought she had been so resourceful, so clever. But she hadn't been clever enough.

Awkwardly, she placed the pad of gauze over the small hole in his shoulder, securing it with the precut adhesive strips. Biting on the inside of her cheek, she began to clean the ragged hole in his back. The only good thing about its presence was that it signaled the bullet had gone through and wasn't lodged in his body.

"You're not exactly running this show, are you, Pennington?" she heard Trace ask through gritted teeth.

"Who, me?" The blond man shook his head. "I'm just following orders."

"A convenient excuse. You won't get away with it."

Pennington tipped his head back and laughed. "I'm just doing my job, trying to capture an agent who's gone bad."

"What's going to happen now, Pennington? Are you going to kill us to save your miserable hide?"

The man looked momentarily startled by Trace's blunt question. "We're taking you down the mountain to a safe house outside of the city. The chief has other plans for you."

"Such as using me as bait, to catch O'Connel?"

The dark blond head snapped up, the pale eyes narrowing, growing small and mean. "Are you finished yet?" he snapped at Emily.

"Almost," she replied tightly. Using a pillowcase one of the men had fetched, she ripped it into strips, wrapping it around the dressing on Logan's lightly tanned chest.

"You did a good job, angel." Trace flexed his shoulder and winced at the pain. Lifting his head, he flashed her a smile that rocked Emily right down to her shoes. It was a bold, broad grin that lacked his habitual cynicism. Black eyes twinkled with mischief, held a hint of promise. "Don't worry, sweetheart, we're not down for the count yet."

Her eyes widened, and she made no protest when Pennington jerked her off of the couch. Surrounded by the men, she and Trace were led out of the cabin. Pennington signaled to a man down the road, and they waited as he fetched a dark maroon car.

The two men holding Trace weren't gentle as they shoved him toward the car. He stumbled over the uneven ground and hit his wounded shoulder on the open door. Emily wrenched herself away from Pennington to go to his aid, only to have the man snatch at her arm.

With fingers curved into claws, she whirled, intent on scratching the man's eyes out if he didn't let her go. Pennington was too quick. He grabbed her and slammed her against the car with enough force to knock the breath right out of her. Her chin hit the top of the car, knocking her teeth together. Blackness threatened to descend over her as bright dots of light danced before her eyes.

For the first time in her life, Emily was terrified that she was going to faint.

Chapter 13

Her head hurt, her chin throbbed, and there was a nasty bruise on her shoulder. She was a mess and felt even worse.

By Emily's loose estimation, she'd had nearly twenty-four hours to reflect on her mistakes, to wonder if she had finally lost her mind. It had to have been twenty-four hours since those men had driven them off of the mountain, had brought them to this large, shadowy house deep in a forest outside of San Francisco. She and Trace had been separated, and Pennington had taken her to this room where she had been locked inside.

She had spent most of that time hunched on a hard cot, trying to think of a way to escape. The door was made out of thick walnut and had been locked the entire time she had been in this small jail cell. Wide iron bars lay over the tiny window. Even the cot had been bolted down to the cement floor.

It was useless. Even if she did manage to escape, she had no idea where to find Trace.

Trace. Emily shoved a hand through her uncombed hair. She had spent hours calling up the image of the broad grin, the black eyes that had danced with mischief. He had called her angel, sweetheart—not honey, or even by her name. She had touched the hard muscles, had gazed upon the light bronze flesh. No matter how crazy it seemed, it hadn't been the same.

Feeling exhausted, mentally, physically and spiritually, she lay back on the thin cot and flung an arm over her eyes. She was going quietly insane, Emily mused, feeling somewhat detached. She had tried to tell herself that she had to be mistaken, that the suspicion and uncertainty were just products of fear, of anger, of defeat.

She hadn't been able to convince herself. No matter how strange, or how crazy it sounded, she was certain that Pennington, for all his bluster, had gotten the wrong man. He looked like Trace, spoke like him, had said all the right things. He had been optimistic, even somewhat cocky as he had tried to reassure her.

That, more than anything, was the final piece of proof that she needed. She wasn't quite sure who Pennington had shot, only that it wasn't Trace Logan.

A scraping noise at the door had Emily jerking herself upright while she held her breath. The door swung open, and admitted a man in an expensive, dark pinstripe suit.

One glance told her that she had never laid eyes on the man who quietly closed the door behind him. Medium-sized, with dark gold hair, the thin-faced man might have been considered quite handsome. Emily didn't care for the weakness she detected around the mouth, or for the cold, dead look in the green-gray eyes.

He was taller than Pennington, his features more delicately etched. They both shared the same cold-blooded look around the eyes. It couldn't be Garibaldi. Jamie had described the head of Control as a dark man with a black soul to match.

Slowly, Emily rose from the bed, making sure her spine was straight. She may feel hopeless and helpless, but she wasn't about to let this man see that. "Who are you?"

His chilling chuckle slithered along her nerve endings, set into her bones. "My name's not important."

She worked hard not to let her fear of this man show on her face. "What do you want?"

"Just some information. Logan's proving to be quite stubborn. I thought you might be more reasonable."

"But I don't know anything."

There was a smug smirk playing around the weak mouth. It was a pity that she didn't have a weapon. Or perhaps it wasn't, she reflected. Otherwise, she might be tempted to do something violent, probably something foolish and dangerous, as well.

"Where's O'Connel?"

Emily shrugged. "I haven't the faintest idea. I haven't seen him since we parted company in Utah."

That awful smile slipped before coming back even colder, harder, with evil intent. "We do have ways of extracting information, Ms. Osborn. Some of them can be quite messy. All of them are most unpleasant."

Emily felt her knees buckle. It was one of the hardest things she had ever done, but she locked them, and willed herself not to falter in front of this man. "It won't help. You can torture me all you want, and you won't find out a thing. I don't have any idea where Jamie is."

The man tipped his head back, and studied her. "Most people aren't aware of what they know. Even if you don't have any information, the only thing it will cost me is some time."

Frantically, Emily searched her mind for a diversion, for something, anything, that would deflect this man from his dreadful course of action. Since physically attacking him would be impossible and dangerous, perhaps a verbal assault would wipe away the man's smug assurance.

"They know who you are," she remarked softly. "They know what you've been doing."

Dark gold brows rose in surprise. The look was covered immediately as the awful smile slipped back into place. "O'Connel and Logan know nothing. They may have suspicions, but I've made sure they're the wrong ones."

Her tongue came out to take a swipe at lips that had gone dust-dry. She had never been very good at verbal fencing, had never tried to be coy, sly or deceitful. She hoped that this one time, she could pull it off.

"I know who you are," she began slowly, trying to inject every bit of self-confidence she possessed into her voice. "If I can figure that out, so can Jamie and Garibaldi."

The thin man swore viciously. He glared at her. It was an evil look, filled with hatred and malice. Emily fought the urge to step away from him.

"If you're so smart, then who am I?"

"The man they call Zeus. The one Pennington has been giving information to."

Maniacal laughter exploded in the room. It came to her with chilling swiftness that this man was insane. Certifiably so. A man that had been riding along the edge for so long, he never realized that he had finally slipped over to the other side.

As surely as the sun was going to rise in the morning, Emily realized she should have never tried to outwit this man. Deep down inside, she knew that she had made a mistake. She couldn't help but worry about how much it was going to cost her.

The thin man stepped forward, and Emily couldn't stop her involuntary movement backward.

"You see, you really do know more than you think you do. You've been told just enough to put it all together—exactly as I had planned."

He advanced, forcing Emily to retreat. When she felt the cold cement wall against her back, she knew there would be no escape.

"You'll never get away with this," she declared as he stopped directly in front of her.

One thin, pale hand rose to encircle her throat. "Oh, but I can, my dear. I already have." His fingers tightened, painfully cutting off her air supply. Emily braced herself, fully prepared to bring her knee up and drive it straight into the most vulnerable part of his body.

She shifted her weight to one foot. A few coldly spoken words stopped her.

"The lady's right. You won't get away with it."

The thin man jerked around, pulling her in front of him. Emily's eyes widened in shock when she spotted the familiar figure standing in the open door. His stance was deceptively casual, his mouth was tilted in a cynical smile. A gun was loosely held in one hand.

"Impossible," the thin man gasped.

"Is it?" Logan retorted coldly. "Hello, Kessler."

Emily felt another jolt rip right through her—all the way down to her toes. Kessler? Wasn't that the name

Trace had said belonged to the man whose body they had found in Jamie's apartment? Searching the familiar, impassive features, she could detect no sign of shock or surprise.

"It can't be," she heard Kessler breathe. "You were locked in. You were shot. I saw you myself."

There was no evidence of a bandage lying under Trace's skintight black T-shirt. Emily hadn't expected to see one.

The cold smile widened. "A lock can hardly contain a ghost." The smile dropped. "Move away from her, Kessler."

"No." The thin man shifted. Emily couldn't help the whimper that escaped when she felt cold hard metal being pressed against her temple. "Drop the gun, Logan."

Every muscle in his body tensed for action. The sight of a gun being held to Emily's head made him furious, scared the hell out of him. Knowing better than to argue, Logan complied. The gun dropped heavily to the floor.

"No," he heard Emily moan, and his hands clenched into tight fists.

Logan warily watched as Kessler's mouth curled into a smug smile. He itched to knock it off of the man's face—with his bare hands. It was all he could do to keep himself from going for the man's throat. Only he couldn't, not while Emily was in the line of fire.

"I wouldn't feel quite so confident if I were you, Kessler. Both Jamie and Garibaldi know about you." Logan allowed himself to feel a measure of satisfaction when Kessler's cockiness slipped.

"You're bluffing."

"They know—" Logan went on in a deadly soft voice that was cloaked in steel "—everything. They know how you used Pennington's gambling debts to force him to pass on information about Control agents. They know how you got him to switch your fingerprints in the files with the ones of an agent named Robbins—just before you blew his face away and dumped his body in Jamie's apartment. They know you've been funneling large amounts of money into an account in the Bahamas. They know it was you who deliberately burned me down in Panama, and then sent an assassin down to make sure I was finished."

"No," Kessler screamed. "They couldn't know." All of the color drained out of the thin face, along with the bravado. It wouldn't do, Logan knew, to push the man too far—not just yet.

"They couldn't know," the shocked man whispered in disbelief. "It was perfect, so perfect."

Logan worked hard to keep a disgusted smile off of his face. Kessler sounded like such a confused little boy, one who had gotten his hand caught in the cookie jar and couldn't understand how it had happened.

"Oh, you were very clever, Kessler."

Emily felt the thin chest behind her puff up in pride. "I took a leaf from your book, Logan. I decided there were certain advantages in rising from the dead."

The man's conceit was incredible, Logan reflected. All of his instincts told him that he should try to take Kessler out now, and not wait for a full confession—before the man did something unpredictable, something crazy. Before he had a chance to hurt Emily.

Logan strained against the restrictions that had been placed on him. He knew he had to keep Kessler talking, keep him off balance—to move him from feeling smug, to feeling totally defeated. There was the matter of finding out the name of the foreign agent who had turned him.

Most important, he had to keep the man's attention away from Emily and directed at him.

Shoving his hands into the pockets of his black jeans, he rocked back on his heels, affecting a careless, almost indolent pose. He needed Kessler to relax, to edge the barrel of the gun away from Emily for just a second. Just one small moment was all he would need.

"It was just too bad you weren't clever enough."

The man blinked, pale eyes growing vague, fuzzy with confusion.

"You may have fooled everyone else into thinking that Robbins was you. But not Jamie," Logan added softly.

"That old man," Kessler dismissed contemptuously. "I've been fooling O'Connel for years."

"Maybe," Logan conceded calmly as he folded his arms over his chest. "But you made two major mistakes."

"Impossible," the man scoffed.

Logan gave him a patronizing smile. "Pennington talked. Loud and clear. It was a mistake to place your trust in a man who would betray his co-workers and friends for a few pieces of silver. You counted on fooling Jamie with another man's body. You can't fool a partner, Kessler," Logan added in a soft tone filled with pity. He shook his head sadly and clicked his tongue. "A partner knows you better than a lover, better than your own mother. He knew, Kessler," he coldly lied. "He knew it wasn't you the minute he saw the body."

"No," Kessler screamed in a horrified denial. "He couldn't have known."

"Oh, but Jamie did. I told you they knew everything," he went on relentlessly. "Everything but why."

Pausing, Logan drew a breath and knew he had to go on. Not because of his orders. He had to know what had made this man become what he was—a traitor, an extortionist, a murderer.

"Why did you do it, Kessler? Was it the money? The excitement? What makes a man sell out his country, sell out his friends? Sell out his soul?"

"Friends?" the man bellowed. "You don't care about the others, only yourself. You want to know why I burned you!"

"Yes."

Harsh, hysterical laughter echoed off the light gray walls. "Because I got sick of hearing how perfect you were. The great Ghostrider," he spat. "That's all I heard from O'Connel. About how good Ghostrider was, how he never made a mistake. Every time things didn't go O'Connel's way, he reminded me that I wasn't you. That no matter how I tried, how hard I worked, I could never be you."

The gun at Emily's head shook, and Logan could see a fanatical light leap into the man's eyes. He was pushing, and Kessler was quickly coming apart at the seams. Any minute now, Logan could make his move.

"Only I knew better." Kessler bragged. "I knew I could beat you. That's why I jumped at the chance when I was approached to hand over some information."

Logan tensed all of his muscles, readied them for action. "Who, Kessler, who approached you?"

"I never bothered to ask him his name. It wasn't important," Kessler dismissed. "The only thing that was important was that he would pay me a rather large sum of money to hand over Ghostrider."

Although Logan itched to get his hands on Kessler, it was most odd, but there was a part of him that pitied the man. It seemed that Kessler had been living so long in the darkness that he no longer recognized the light.

There was, Logan decided, one sure way to get the man to remove the gun from Emily's head. Cocking his head, he thoughtfully stroked his cheek. "It's a pity you failed, Kessler. Didn't it occur to you just how hard it would be to trap a ghost?"

"I never believed any of that hokum." The voice may have been calm, but the way the gun shook ever so slightly, Logan knew that Kessler was anything but calm. Just a few more minutes, that was all he needed. Just a few minutes more.

"You should have believed," Logan taunted in a silky-smooth voice. "You should have listened to them. Locks and walls can't hold a ghost. You can't shoot a man who's already dead."

"No," Kessler screamed. "You're not some damn ghost. You're just a man. A man!" Again, loud, maniacal laughter filled the room as he waved the gun in the air. "You may have believed all that stuff. And it's going to be the death of you. I can prove you're just a man."

Emily had gone limp when the gun had been removed from her head. Now she stiffened in horror. She couldn't believe that Trace was daring the man to shoot him. She couldn't believe that Kessler would not do it, either. And do it gladly.

Clenching her teeth, she knew that she wasn't about to let that happen.

"You're going to die, Logan. And there'll be no resurrection this time." The gun was leveled at Logan.

She clawed at the arm that was pressed against her throat. Lifting her foot, she stamped hard on the man's shoe. Kessler screamed in pain, in rage.

Emily's struggle was just the diversion that Logan had been waiting for. He jumped, tucking his body into a ball, and rolled into the two struggling people. They went down in a tangle of arms and legs.

Freeing himself, Logan lunged at Kessler. He pushed an arm over the man's throat and grabbed his wrist. Slamming it hard against the floor, he grunted in satisfaction when Kessler dropped the gun.

Looking down into the pale eyes, Logan smiled. "I told you that you couldn't kill a ghost."

Kessler went limp in defeat and Logan knew that it was all over.

Waves of pain shot through Emily's shoulder to lodge in her skull. The room swam before her eyes and it suddenly seemed filled with dozens of people. The light was blotted out when a familiar dark head filled her vision.

"Emily? Are you hurt?"

"Trace?" Pain slashed through her when she tried to lift her arm. She must have hit her bruised shoulder when she'd hit the floor.

"I'm okay, I think. Are you all right?"

He reached over to tenderly cup her cheek. "I'm fine, Emily. It's all over."

She looked over Trace's shoulder to see a subdued Kessler being escorted out of the room by two men. The first man with the swarthy complexion was a stranger. The red-headed giant she knew.

Emily saw the piece of white tape that lay on the broad nose, saw the signs of swelling under the mist-blue eyes. How had Jamie gotten hurt? she wondered.

Trace helped her to stand and sat her down on the edge of the cot. He ran his hands over her, making sure, Emily supposed, that she had told him the truth that she wasn't hurt. "How is it that you came to my rescue this time?"

Logan grasped her hands and laced his fingers through hers. "I had a hard time shaking those men who were on my trail in Utah, so I was late getting to the airport. I made it to the cabin just in time to see Pennington take you away."

He couldn't stop touching her. He still had those feelings of helplessness, of rage. It had been touch and go for him when he had seen them leave the cabin, and he hadn't been able to follow. It had been worse seeing her being held by Kessler. Logan wasn't sure that he was going to be able to let her go.

"I tracked down Garibaldi and was relieved to find out that he was keeping tabs on Pennington. We placed a stakeout around this place and nabbed him as he was leaving."

"So Garibaldi wasn't a traitor after all."

Logan stroked a hand down her arm. "No. It was like Jamie and I figured. He just used us to flush out the leak."

"How did you find out that Kessler was still alive?"

"Pennington was all too willing to talk to save his hide. He was heavily in debt and needed the money Kessler was willing to pay him. He switched the fingerprints in the file to make us think that Kessler was dead. Then, on Kessler's orders, he directed his men to find Jamie and me."

"So there were more people involved in this than just Pennington and Kessler."

"Not directly," Logan countered. "Except for the two men who broke into the motel room that first night, the rest all thought they were just doing their jobs. Garibaldi had those two, plus the Scaffers, picked up this morning after Pennington confessed."

Emily shuddered at the thought of her refined neighbors being a part of the murderous plot. "Then the Scaffers knew about the trap?"

Logan's mouth flattened into a hard line. "Kessler offered them enough money to retire in style."

The thought of the elegant Dorothea Scaffer spending time in jail was horrible. Emily hardened her heart. The neighbors she had always considered to be so nice had been willing to betray their country, had been willing to be a party to murder—for money.

Emily sighed. The nightmare was finally over, and except for a few bumps and bruises, they all were basically fine. She reached for him to assure herself that he was all right, only to gasp when the pain hit her again.

"You *are* hurt," Logan rasped. "You need to go to the hospital and get checked out.

"It's just a few bruises. I'm fine really, now that I know this whole thing is finally over."

He dipped his head, and she could feel the tension in the hands that tightened around hers. An ominous feeling spread through her.

"It is for you. Since Kessler claims he doesn't know the name of the man he was selling information to, then the job isn't over."

Emily's heart dropped to the pit of her stomach. She had forgotten what Jamie had told her in that dismal garage in Utah. The job wasn't over—not for Ghostrider. Would it ever be?

It was, she realized, only over for her—in more ways than one. She had been right before. There was no future in loving a ghost.

As he helped her up off the cot, Emily fought against a wave of dizziness. Looking up into his concerned eyes, she suddenly recalled another pair of dancing black eyes.

"Trace," she began slowly. "If you only arrived at the cabin when we were leaving, then who was that man who came before? Who did Pennington shoot?"

A rueful smile touched his lips as he lifted his hand and signaled in the direction of a group of men. One man detached himself from the group and Emily could only stare in astonishment.

"Emily, I'd like you to meet my brother."

Her manners forgotten, she could only gape at the man whose face was a mirror image of Trace Logan.

Chapter 14

There was danger in the darkness. And terror. She wanted to run, to hide, but her feet wouldn't move. High, harsh laughter echoed through the night, and the sound of footsteps drawing ever closer made her feel trapped, helpless. Emily whimpered.

A soft, sweet voice called to her, a soothing sound that overpowered the fear. She fought the grasping tentacles that tried to draw her back into the dream.

Emily opened her eyes. Focusing on the shadowy face looming over her, she looked directly into a pair of worried eyes. They were every bit as intense as she remembered, but now they were not cloaked or impassive. She could read the turbulent emotion in them, see the concern in the grim twist of that beautiful mouth.

Trace. It all came back to her in a rush—the small cramped room, the madness that had been let loose.

"It's all right, honey. It's just a dream. You're going to be just fine."

She tried to smile, only to find that the muscles in her mouth wouldn't obey her. Her lashes drifted down, and she fought against the medication that had been given to her earlier.

Forcing her eyes open, she tried to make the words come. They came out as a groan.

"Don't try to talk," Logan soothed. "You're going to be just fine, I promise you."

The weight on her lashes proved too much and they fluttered down. From deep inside, Emily mustered whatever strength was left and finally managed to speak.

"I love you," she croaked, just as sleep claimed her once again.

The next thing Emily became aware of was a healing warmth on her cheek, the soft rustling sounds of movement. She felt groggy, disoriented.

Bright sunlight assaulted her eyes, and Emily fought the urge to slam them shut. It wasn't hard to fight, especially when she spied the figure hunched uncomfortably in the chair that had been placed next to the bed.

"I'm so glad you're all right," she murmured softly.

The man returned her smile. "Me too, sweetheart."

Emily lowered her lashes in confusion. It wasn't that lazy, cynical smile she had actually grown so fond of. It was too warm, too open, too free of shadows. "Trace?"

Leaning forward, the man clasped her hand. "No, angel, I'm not Trace. I'm—"

"Tyler." The name just slipped out from her subconscious where it had been lingering for quite some time.

"So you do remember my name. The way Trace hustled us both to the hospital, I wasn't sure if he even mentioned it."

"Trace told me a little about you before. Very little," Emily mused wryly. "It seemed he left out the most important fact."

"That we're twins?" His smile widened. "I'm not surprised. I've been Trace's closely guarded secret for years."

Twins. She could hardly take it in. This man was the spitting image of Trace. Almost. It was like seeing an image of what Trace might have looked like had he lived a different kind of life.

Especially around the eyes. They were just as dark, just as compelling. But they were gentler, more open, more easily read. He appeared younger, less abused by life. Tyler Logan wasn't as lean, hard or cynical as his brother. He was softer, less intense, smoother around the edges.

Emily couldn't believe that she had ever mistaken this man for Trace. "I suppose that you are a spy, too?"

Even his laughter was different. It sounded happy, free and not at all forced or contained. "No, I'm not. I'm a cop."

Her brow wrinkled. "Then how did you get mixed up in all of this?"

He lifted one shoulder. "Jamie O'Connel called me. Said Trace needed me to look after a very special package that was at the cabin."

"But I thought...Trace said..." She shook her head. "I thought you believed Trace had died in that plane crash."

Tyler's expression turned hard, grim. A shiver raced down her spine. She had been wrong. There were times when this man was exactly like Trace.

"I did. For two years I thought I'd lost my brother."

Her fingers clutched the sheet as she felt the man's pain. How could Trace have done it? How could he have cut himself off from his family, from Tyler, a man who had probably been closer to him than just a brother?

Like a balloon bursting, she saw that white-hot anger suddenly deflate, leaving the man with Trace's face looking older, tired and world-weary. He wasn't quite as adept as his brother at hiding his feelings. Emily watched as several conflicting emotions passed over the sharply handsome face—hurt, anger and finally acceptance.

"So Trace did tell you the truth."

"No." He shifted in the chair, a spasm of pain chasing through his eyes. "A man called Garibaldi approached me, and told me such an incredible tale I called him a liar. You see, up until then, I thought Trace was working for an engineering firm."

A ghost of a smile drifted over his lips. "He told me Trace was in trouble and needed my help."

"To spy for him?" she burst out in astonishment.

"Nothing quite so dramatic, or dangerous. He just wanted me to be Trace for a while."

That certainly explained how Tyler had known who Pennington was, Emily reflected. The bits and pieces of the conversation between Jamie and Trace back in Utah, suddenly fell into place. Garibaldi must have used Tyler for some underhanded scheme, and Trace must have been furious.

It must have been so terribly difficult for this man to accept. Outrage must have warred with love and the loyalty he felt for a man who had shared the same womb with him for nine months.

"That must have come as a shock."

He gave her that quick easy smile that was so vastly different from Trace's slow hard one. "It was and it wasn't. Deep down, I don't think I really believed Trace was gone."

For two years, Tyler had been told his brother was dead. Only to find out it had been a lie. That the man he had trusted, loved and grieved for, had deliberately deceived him.

"I suppose Trace was furious when he found out that Jamie had involved you."

That easy grin turned softer. "I doubt O'Connel's nose will ever be the same. Actually, to give the man his due, I don't suppose O'Connel believed that he was placing me in any danger by sending me up to see you."

Was that how Jamie had gotten hurt, because Trace had punched him in the nose? Emily thought, remembering the piece of tape that had decorated Jamie's nose.

Her gaze went to Tyler as she searched for the bandage hidden under the navy blue shirt. No danger? To give Tyler his due, it must have taken a gigantic leap of faith, of trust, to help the brother who had lied to him. He had even taken a bullet that had been meant for Trace.

"What I don't understand is why Kessler or Pennington didn't put it together and realize that they had shot you, not Trace."

"That's easy." Tyler leaned back, resting one ankle over his knee. "They never knew about me. When Trace moved into Control, his records were sealed. The only people who knew that he was Trace Logan were O'Connel and Garibaldi. He was a man without a name or a past."

"A ghost," she supplied thoughtfully.

So all the pieces had finally come together. It would take, she decided, a very long time for her to come to terms with them. There was just one more thing she had to know.

Once again, she found herself digging into the reserves of her strength. She was afraid of asking, knew she could no longer bear not knowing. "Where's Trace?"

That look of soft sympathy was almost more than she could bear. "He's gone, Emily. Back to Washington. There's still some loose ends to tie up."

"Yes, I suppose there would be," she murmured faintly, desperately trying to hold back the tears of loss. This grueling ordeal was over—for her. Trace still had a job to do, tracking down a spy.

She should have been filled with relief. The only thing Emily felt was a crushing depression. Trace was gone, off placing himself in danger, perhaps some day to be...

Emily buried that gruesome thought, wishing she had gotten to say goodbye. She never had the opportunity to thank him for helping her to see that deep inside of her was a woman of strength.

Tyler dug into his pocket and withdrew a white envelope, offering it to her. Emily didn't want to touch it. She was afraid she already knew what it said.

"Trace wanted me to give this to you." He placed the letter on the bed.

"Emily..." He was cut short as a plump nurse bustled into the room.

"Ah, you're awake, Ms. Osborn. That's good." Lifting her arm slightly off of the bed, the nurse placed two stout fingers on the inside of Emily's wrist as she shot Tyler a hard look. "You were supposed to ring when Ms. Osborn was awake. You'll have to leave now."

"But..."

"No buts, Mr. Logan. You remember our deal," the woman retorted in a tone that would brook no disobedience.

Casting a helpless look at Emily, Tyler shrugged. "I'll see you later."

Emily could only manage a faint smile. She didn't want to see Tyler later. She didn't want to see anyone. She just wanted to wallow in her misery, in the knowledge that Trace was gone, and that it hadn't been him last night who had whispered those soft words of comfort.

Dully, dutifully, Emily allowed herself to be poked and prodded. Her eyes kept drifting over to the letter the nurse had placed on the high table next to the bed.

Finally, once she was alone, she picked up the envelope. As she scanned the contents, Emily willed herself not to cry. It was an apology for involving her in the nightmare. It was a plea for her not to think too badly of him. It was a note of goodbye.

Emily wanted to get angry. She wanted to weep. She wanted to go home.

Her dismal thoughts were interrupted by the sound of a very loud, very angry, very familiar voice outside of her room.

"Patient. I've been the picture of patience and cooperation. My patience is at an end. I want to see Emily!"

She wondered who was going to win the battle of wills. That dragon of a nurse or the equally hardheaded man who was demanding to see her.

Her answer came when the man burst through the door. The loud, flowered shirt he wore gave Emily a headache, and along with the white linen pants, he was a too-vivid reminder of another, darker man.

Planting his hands on his hips, the man glared at her. "Well, this is one fine mess you've gotten yourself into."

Much to her astonishment, Emily burst into tears. In seconds, she felt those strong arms go around her. "Oh please, Em, don't cry. It's going to be all right."

She was sure it would never be all right. Emily lifted her tear-stained face. "Please take me home, Luke. I want to go home."

Emily stepped out onto the hot pavement and felt the searing heat beat down on her. In the month since Luke had brought her home, Phoenix had just gotten hotter. The summer monsoon season that was supposed to help cool off the city, had failed to materialize. Everyone was still suffering under triple-digit temperatures.

Ignoring the blast of heat, Emily reached into her oversized purse and plucked out a pair of sunglasses. Placing them over her eyes, she headed toward her car. A small smile crept over her mouth when she spotted the shiny red sports car.

On a mad impulse, she had gotten rid of her old reliable Ford, had replaced it with this smaller, sportier model. She had ruthlessly gone through her wardrobe and had rooted out all of her dull, predictable clothes. They had been replaced with bolder garments, all in shades of lavender and complementary colors.

Changes, Emily reflected as she slid into the driver's seat. There had been plenty of those. Although she had dyed her hair back to its original color, not much else had remained the same. Once she had returned home, she had made arrangements to take the last week of her vacation. Hawaii had been lovely, only she hadn't appreciated the breathtaking scenery. It hadn't felt exotic or exciting, merely lonely.

The minute she had returned from her vacation, she had decided to open a second bookstore and had plunged into that new venture with both feet.

Even her parents' attitude had changed toward her. They still didn't approve of the way she lived her life, but they had started looking at her with a new respect.

It had been Luke who'd had a hard time accepting the changes. He had been wonderful, supportive of her decision to open a second bookstore, which she appreciated. He also hovered too much, which she didn't care for.

He had been understanding about what she had done when she had been with Trace. Unfortunately, he kept pressing for details. Except for one night shortly after they had gotten back to Phoenix when she had pitifully poured out some of the sorry mess to her disbelieving brother, she hadn't mentioned another word about Trace Logan.

She hadn't wanted to talk about him, hadn't wanted to become morose or maudlin. She hadn't wanted to keep dwelling on that short, but terribly important part of her life. She hadn't wanted to forget.

Emily turned the key in the ignition, and paused for a moment to listen to the powerful growl of the engine. She sighed. It too reminded of her of Trace.

The only thing predictable in her life was that she hadn't heard from him. Not one word. Jamie had sent her flowers, along with a sweet card and a personal note. It was through him that she had found out that Kessler, along with the Scaffers, was going to go on trial in a few weeks.

Tyler had phoned three times from his home in Seattle to make sure that she was all right. Although the conversations had been pleasant and friendly, she hadn't really wanted to talk to a man who so closely reminded her of Trace.

She had even had a strange, uncomfortable visit from Ray Garibaldi. Trace's boss had turned out to be the small, swarthy man she had seen escorting Kessler away. She had taken an instant dislike to him. The white roses he had brought had seemed cold, impersonal. Perhaps, Emily mused, because she had seen the flowers as a reflection of the man.

The drive home was short. Pulling the sports car into the dark, cramped area of her garage, she bent and retrieved her purse and briefcase. Pushing the button that would close the wide door, she slipped the key into the lock on the connecting kitchen door. Another thing that hadn't changed was her habit of placing her briefcase and purse on top of the small table sitting in the alcove with the bay window.

She never made it. Strong arms came from behind, one sliding around her chest, pinning her arms to her side. One roughly callused hand glided over her mouth as she was hauled back against a body that was as hard, as unyielding as a block of granite. Stunned, the only thing Emily could think of was, *Oh, no, not again.*

Instinctively, she struggled against the assailant, even though she knew that he was far too strong for her pitiful attempts.

"Don't, Emily. Don't be scared. It's only me."

Instantly, Emily was struck by a blinding fury. She jerked out of her assailant's arms and turned, her hands balling into fists. "You! You scared the bewillies out of me, Trace Logan!"

Leaning one hip against the marbled counter, he casually folded his arms over his broad chest. He looked good. Too good. It was impossible for her to believe that Trace was here. She wished he hadn't come.

Fighting the softening inside of her, Emily braced herself for battle. "Why can't you use the doorbell to announce your presence—like a normal person?"

"I wanted to see you. I wasn't sure you'd let me in."

At first glance, Trace looked the same, self-assured, confident and fully in control. But he wasn't. Looking deeply into his eyes, she saw they were alive with swirling emotions. He looked ill at ease, almost afraid.

"Why?" she demanded.

"It's quite simple really, Emily. I found I can't live without you."

White-hot rage burned inside of her. "You certainly lived without me all these weeks. You dumped me in the hospital without a word. I heard from everyone and their mother, but not from you. You expect me to believe that you can't live without me?"

Slowly, he straightened away from the counter. "I didn't just dump you in the hospital, Emily. I had to leave."

"Because you had to finish the job," she retorted hotly.

She wasn't, Logan could see, going to make this easy for him. After the abrupt way he had left her, he hadn't really expected Emily to make it easy.

During those long, frustrating weeks when he was trying to uncover Zeus's identity, he had been miserable. He had told himself that he was being noble, was doing the right thing. He was leaving Emily alone to find a man that was more worthy of her.

He thought about her constantly during the emotional reunion with his parents. All during his week-long stay, he'd seen the love shared by his mother and father, saw how they had supported each other. And Logan had known he wanted that same thing with Emily.

He knew he was a selfish man because he couldn't bear the thought of another man receiving all that love and trust. Emily Osborn was a woman worth wooing, worth winning. If she would have him, Logan knew that nothing was going to stop him from going to her, from having her—except Emily herself.

Bracing himself, Logan spoke. "I told myself that it was better that way. No goodbyes, just a clean break. It tore me apart to leave, only I had to, because of you."

Emotions, like fallen leaves scattering in the wind, skidded across her face. That small pink tongue came out to moisten her lips. "Why because of me?"

"Finding you, being with you, taught me that there was still honor, nobility and trust left in the world. I knew I had to honor my commitment to my job, keep my word to Garibaldi, and my promise to you."

Logan paused, one hand coming to rest at the back of his neck as he tried to tease out some of the tension, some of the fear that had gathered there.

"I told myself that you could never live in my world, that you might try and it would end up destroying you. I convinced myself that you deserved better than me, someone cleaner, more open—" a rueful smile drifted over his lips "—more honest."

He stepped closer, fighting the urge to hold her and convince her of his feelings in a more direct, more physical way. "All the time that I was searching for some clue to Zeus's identity, I told myself that the best thing I could do for you was to stay away, never darken your doorstep again. In the end, I knew I couldn't. Because of the very last thing you told me."

Raising a hand to her forehead, Emily rubbed it, trying to remember. Those few moments were hazy. She could remember Trace taunting the man, daring him to shoot. She could recall being more frightened than she'd ever been in her life, being determined not to let any harm come to Trace.

She couldn't remember what she had said when Trace had bundled her into the car that would take her to the hospital. She could only remember the crushing depression that had fallen over her.

"You were having a nightmare," he went on softly. "Trying to fight against the sleeping pill you had been given. You smiled at me, Emily. You told me you loved me."

Anger, relief, confusion, joy all warred inside of her. "You were there," she whispered rawly.

"I was there. I came by to see for myself that you were all right. I stayed with you because I couldn't bear to leave until I had to."

"You really were there."

"Despite all the debating I've done with myself over the past weeks, I knew I'd be back."

"Why?"

He reached for her, his long, slim fingers cupping her face. "I love you, Emily. You are the light in my life. You taught me how to trust, how to hope, how to dream again." He lowered his head, and brushed a light kiss over her trembling lips.

"I want to share my life with you," he murmured fiercely. "All the joys, the sorrows. I want to share children with you. I'm a selfish man. I want it all."

Briefly, her lashes dipped down to shield herself from those mesmerizing eyes. Trace was offering her everything she had wished for, hoped for, dreamed about.

And she knew she couldn't accept it. It nearly tore her heart apart.

"Will you marry me, Emily?"

"I can't," she whispered in misery.

Trace looked stricken, as if she had just slapped him in the face. He looked resigned, as if he had expected nothing else.

"It's your fault, Trace Logan," she went on gently. "You see, I finally believe what you tried to tell me. That I'm strong enough to do what has to be done."

She folded her hands together, to keep herself from reaching for him. "I love you. But I'm strong enough to realize that I can't share you with a job that takes you into such danger. It nearly killed me to get on that bus in Utah, knowing you were going off, perhaps to get yourself killed. I nearly died when I saw that madman pointing a gun at you, intending to shoot."

Emily swallowed hard, tasted the tears that were flowing freely down her pale cheeks. "You see, I'm selfish, too."

She expected almost anything but that slow, lazy grin that spread over his beautiful mouth. "A woman after my own heart. We're going to do very well together, Emily."

"But..."

"There's no longer a department called Control. With three of its agents dead, one of the key people under arrest and my cover blown, there isn't a department any longer." He brushed another kiss across her lips. "I quit, Emily. I handed in my resignation the day I found out Zeus's identity and turned it over to Garibaldi."

"You quit your job?" she squeaked, not able to restrain the brilliant smile that stole over her mouth.

"They've had ten years of my life. The last six, they've owned me body and soul." He shrugged. "I told you I was a selfish man. I want it all now. I want you."

Emily barely hesitated as she tossed her arms around his neck. Trace lifted her off her feet, sweeping an arm under her knees.

"Do you think you can marry a man who's now unemployed?"

She tightened her arms around his neck. "As long as I know you'll be safe, I'll take you anyway I can get you."

Trace carried her along the short hall to the bedroom. It brought back images of the last time he had dragged her through her house. Then, she had been so frightened, so unsure of herself. She had come a long way since that night. A very long way. From being a helpless, frightened victim, to a woman who was trusted and relied on, to one that was loved and needed.

Trace gently laid her on the bed, his hands deftly removing her clothes. "It's been so long, honey, I don't think I can hold out."

There was a trembling need in his voice, the light of love shining in his eyes. Emily reached up and pulled him down to her. "I don't think I can wait, either. I'm not only a selfish woman, I'm a greedy one, too."

It wasn't a half smile he gave her, full of cynicism and weariness. It was a vibrant smile, one filled with joy. "We're going to be better than good together." He buried his face between her breasts. "I promise you, I'll take care of you, Emily. I'll protect you, keep you safe."

Tunneling her fingers through his silky black hair, she lifted his head. "I don't need you to protect me, Trace. Not since the time a very special man showed me that I could be a woman of strength, a woman that could do what she had to do. I only need you.''

Hands encircled her breasts, tempting her aching nipples into pebbled points. ''You need someone to stand beside you, to hold you when you cry, to laugh with you when you're happy, to watch over you when you're vulnerable. Just as I need a woman of strength to do those things for me.''

Nothing ever felt so wonderful, so right as when Trace slid inside of her. Looking up at those dark eyes, Emily saw for the first time that they were open, not cloaked, impassive or unreadable. Gone were the shadows that had haunted him during the time they had been together. No longer did he seem the dark, driven man she had first seen in the bright light of her bathroom.

As they moved together in the dying of the afternoon light, Emily knew that Ghostrider was gone. Logan, her beloved Trace, was here to stay.

As they both reached for the pot of gold at the end of the rainbow, Emily knew she was no longer just a dreamer of dreams. She was living them. And that the man who had been running for his life, had finally come home.

Epilogue

A silent Emily stood over the crib in the gaily decorated nursery, and stared down at the sleeping miracle of Tracy Hope Logan. Named for her father, this small scrap of humanity was a living testament that dreams do come true.

Pulling up the pink blanket over the tiny form, Emily couldn't help the funny smile that stole over her face. She was always staring at this miracle child, found a thousand and one excuses to touch her. It had been three months since they had brought this little bundle to the home Trace had built with his own hands, and Emily still had to pinch herself to make sure this wasn't a dream.

Happiness flooded through her. Without her ever hearing a sound, strong arms came from behind to capture her. Emily felt herself sink back into the loving embrace.

"Are you going to stare at the baby all night, honey?"

"I could," she replied in a low whisper. "She's so beautiful."

"That's because she takes after her mother," Trace remarked with a low chuckle.

"Not with all that gorgeous black hair." Emily turned her mouth, placing a light kiss across his whisker-rough jaw.

"Ah, but she has your mouth, and already those baby-blues are turning light."

It was a familiar, friendly argument, one they had had several times since they had brought Tracy home from the hospital.

"Well, as beautiful as this kid is, you have to go to bed. You have to work in the morning."

Emily pulled away. "You have classes to go to," she reminded him. If anyone had told her a year and a half ago that she would be married to an ex-spy who, at the age of thirty-four, had returned to school to earn his advanced degree in architectural engineering, she would never have believed them.

"Not until noon," Trace replied as he placed feather-light kisses on the back of her neck.

"Well, Brent is going to take over for a few days, so I can spend some time with my husband and my daughter."

Since she and Trace had married, she had made Brent Conway more of her personal assistant than merely the manager of one of her two bookstores. He had been a godsend, even though Trace had not taken kindly to the fact she had to work so closely with the man.

He had always said he was a selfish man. Trace Logan was also a possessive one. And Emily wouldn't have him any other way.

"Well, I'm glad Conway is good for something," he teased. He gave her a slow, sexy smile that sent her pulse racing.

Emily moved out of his arms, and slowly walked over to the door. Pausing, she gave him a smoldering look. "Well, why don't we start now?"

Logan immediately felt his body grow hard, and excited. He moved after his wife, only to pause at the doorway to give one last glance at the small sleeping figure in the crib.

All at once, he realized that he had stopped running from the past, from all the regrets and the remorse. He had started racing toward the future. Logan smiled softly. He had a feeling that the wife he adored, that the marvelous daughter she had given him, were going to give him a run for his money.

Emily had healed the old hurts, and the scars from the past. Tracy had taught him the meaning of the word *hope*. He was a lucky man. A very lucky man who probably didn't deserve either one of them.

Logan flipped on the nightlight.

"Trace?" The sound of that sleepy, sexy voice had him hotfooting it down the hall into the master bedroom he had lovingly created for Emily. Seeing her stretched out on the king-size bed without a stitch of clothing, Logan knew he was a very lucky man indeed. Because he had Emily.

Ghostrider had been laid to rest. Now there was only Trace Logan, devoted husband and proud father. A man with a past, a present and an incredibly brilliant future in the light.

*   *   *   *   *

TAKE A WALK ON THE DARK SIDE OF LOVE

October is the shivery season, when chill winds blow and shadows walk the night. Come along with us into a haunting world where love and danger go hand in hand, where passions will thrill you and dangers will chill you. Come with us to

In this newest short story collection from Sihouette Books, three of your favorite authors tell tales just perfect for a spooky autumn night. Let Anne Stuart introduce you to "The Monster in the Closet," Helen R. Myers bewitch you with "Seawitch," and Heather Graham Pozzessere entice you with "Wilde Imaginings."

Silhouette Shadows™
Haunting a store near you this October.

In the spirit of Christmas, Silhouette invites
you to share the joy of the holiday season.

Experience the beauty of Yuletide romance with Silhouette
Christmas Stories 1992—a collection of heartwarming stories by
favorite Silhouette authors.

JONI'S MAGIC by Mary Lynn Baxter
HEARTS OF HOPE by Sondra Stanford
THE NIGHT SANTA CLAUS RETURNED by Marie Ferrarella
BASKET OF LOVE by Jeanne Stephens

This Christmas you can also receive a FREE keepsake Christmas
ornament. Look for details in all November and December
Silhouette books.

Also available this year are three popular early editions of
Silhouette Christmas Stories—1986, 1987 and 1988. Look for these
and you'll be well on your way to a complete collection of the
best in holiday romance.

Share in the celebration—with Silhouette's
Christmas gift of love.

SX92